"While we're on the subject of getting things straight...I don't regret kissing you, Vanessa. Quite the contrary." That curious gleam swam again in his eyes. "Would it surprise you to hear I'd like to do it again?"

A hot jet of arousal flashed through her veins. For a moment she was so shaken she couldn't respond. She wet her suddenly dry lips, then wished she hadn't. She didn't want to give him the wrong idea.

Her voice was a croak. "That wouldn't be wise."

The line between his brows gradually deepened. "You're right. Of course. Not wise at all."

She gazed up dreamily, lost in the entrancing mirrors of his eyes. "So was that kiss just part of the service?"

His jaw tightened. "No. That was unforgivable. It won't happen again."

"You're certain?"

The pad of his thumb grazed her lips before his mouth descended once more. "Absolutely."

What do you look for in a guy? Charisma. Sex appeal. Confidence. A body to die for. Looks that stand out from the crowd. Well, look no further—the heroes in this miniseries have all this, and more! And now that they've met the women in these novels, there is one thing on everyone's mind....

NIGHTS *of* PASSION

One night is never enough!

These guys know what they want and how they're going to get it!

Don't miss any of these hot stories, where romance and sizzling passion are guaranteed!

Robyn Grady

NAUGHTY NIGHTS IN THE MILLIONAIRE'S MANSION

NIGHTS *of* PASSION

One night is never enough!

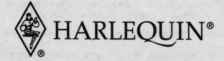

HARLEQUIN®

TORONTO • NEW YORK • LONDON
AMSTERDAM • PARIS • SYDNEY • HAMBURG
STOCKHOLM • ATHENS • TOKYO • MILAN • MADRID
PRAGUE • WARSAW • BUDAPEST • AUCKLAND

Recycling programs
for this product may
not exist in your area.

ISBN-13: 978-0-373-12850-1

NAUGHTY NIGHTS IN THE MILLIONAIRE'S MANSION

First North American Publication 2009.

Copyright © 2009 by Robyn Grady.

www.eHarlequin.com

Printed in U.S.A.

All about the author...
Robyn Grady

One Christmas long ago, **ROBYN GRADY** received a book from her big sister and immediately fell in love with the story of Cinderella. Sprinklings of magic, deepest wishes coming true—she was hooked! Picture books with glass slippers later gave way to romance novels and, more recently, the real-life dream of writing for Harlequin Books.

After a fifteen-year career in television, Robyn met her own modern-day hero. They live on Australia's Sunshine Coast with their three little princesses, two poodles and a cat called Tinkie. Robyn loves new shoes, worn jeans, lunches at Moffat Beach and hanging out with her friends on eHarlequin.com. Learn about her latest releases at www.robyngrady.com, and don't forget to say hi. She'd love to hear from you!

To Moet and Ebony, with love

CHAPTER ONE

'It's settled. You're coming home with me.'

The low murmur at Vanessa Craig's back left her nape tingling, as if her skin had been brushed by an intimate kiss. Drawn from stacking the last of the special diet dog food, she curled some hair behind her ear, then slowly edged around. She tried—but failed—to keep her eyes in her head.

Of course, the attractive man standing nearby hadn't spoken to her. Heck, he didn't know she existed, even if Vanessa was acutely aware of every sensitised cell in her body suddenly glowing with life.

Powerhouse height, pitch-black hair, a strong shadowed jaw and eyes bluer than any Vanessa had seen. The precise cut of his trousers, the immaculate polish of his shoes—everything about this man didn't simply say he settled for the best.

He *was* the best.

When the man-god shifted his weight, the ledge of his magnificent shoulders went back. His attention drifted from the small tank, which contained a single goldfish, and landed on her.

'Afternoon.' His mouth curved up at one side as he quarter-turned to face her. 'You work here?'

Vanessa swallowed the knot of hot desire tugging in her throat. 'I'm the manager.'

'Great. I'm interested in that fish.'

Vanessa studied the goldfish, who was busy studying the man. She smiled over. 'Not half as interested as he seems to be in *you*.'

While she spoke, the light changed in her customer's ocean-blue eyes, as though something in her face or her voice, made him wonder if they'd met before. Not on this side of her dreams.

As his sexy smile returned, he tilted his head at the tank. 'I'm wondering…can you tell his gender?'

Although Vanessa had answered that question regarding fish many times in the past two years, the majority of people who visited her Sydney pet store— Great and Small—seemed content to while away some time fawning over the puppies and kittens. Who could blame them? Cute bundles of fur bouncing around, pressing their squishy wet noses against the window, desperate for a cuddle. Searching for a home.

Caring for her animals was a labour of pure love, but the real joy came when one went to a family whom she knew would truly care. Friends were great: Josie and Tia, her buddies since high school, were the best. But family, *real* family…well, everybody wanted one.

Did this man have a family? Was he an uncle? A father?

She set a hand on a corner of the cool tank. 'Males can have tiny dots on the gills and pectoral fins. Like those.' She waggled a finger at the little guy's fins, then filtered in an interesting detail. 'Did you know that the Japanese have been keeping goldfish as pets for over a thousand years?'

His gorgeous eyes smiled and sparkled. 'Is that right?'

She nodded. 'It's also a bona fide fact that watching fish swim can be soothing to the nerves.'

'Well, that's got to be cheaper than the psychiatrist I'm seeing.'

Vanessa's jaw dropped, but then he lifted a brow and smiled—a sultry *gotcha* smile that burrowed beneath the skin and coddled every inch of her.

'Actually, a friend of mine has a large aquarium,' he admitted. 'He says nothing's more relaxing at the end of a long, hard day. No fuss, no bother. No noise.' The impressive breadth of his chest expanded beneath its dark wool blend shirt as he retrieved his wallet from a back pocket. 'Do you take Visa?'

But before he could extract the card, his attention shifted to a nearby glass pen and its excited scramble of Rottweiler pups. Aware her scent was Perfume de la Birdcage from the tray she'd cleaned earlier, Vanessa swiped both hands down her jeans and moved closer. 'They're pretty special, huh? Only came in this morning.'

When the lines of his classically cut profile intensified, as if he were considering a change of tack, she subtly tested, 'Have you owned a dog before?'

Attention fixed on the pups, the dark slashes of his brows fell together. 'I grew up with dogs…' His Hollywood jaw shifted. 'Kind of.'

She grinned. 'Kind of grew up, or kind of dogs?'

His crystalline gaze met hers again; the contact rippled through her blood like the aftermath of a fiery liquid touch.

'Poodles.' His gaze dipped to her mouth, traced the sweep of her lips, then flicked back to her eyes. 'I grew up with poodles. The tiny, yappy ones.'

Only half recovered from the sizzle of his gaze, she dug her hands into her pockets and rocked back on her Reeboks. 'Whatever size, poodles are a highly intelligent breed.'

'They certainly know how to get what they want.'

'The family pooches were pampered?'

'Like every other female in the house.' His brows crunched together again. 'Sorry. Too much information.'

She didn't mind. She was intrigued.

So he had a mother as well as sisters, sounded like. The fine lines branching from the corners of his eyes said late twenties, early thirties at the outside—too old to live at home with the brood. Had he grown up overrun by female siblings and a domineering matriarch? Perhaps his father had been away often, a foreign diplomat for some exotic far-off land; the dreamy slant to his eyes and coal-fringed lashes suggested a Mediterranean connection maybe.

She smiled at herself.

And maybe she needed to get a life. Whatever his

background, she wouldn't get to know him well enough to hear it.

'These pups are only eight weeks old. They'll grow a whole lot bigger. I'd suggest a good quality bed.' She selected one from a nearby display. 'We recommend this brand.'

Close to where her hand rested, he rubbed and pinched the foam. 'Hmm. Firm yet soft.'

As if on direct dial, the tips of her breasts picked up, tightening to responsive beads beneath her T-shirt. Vanessa surrendered to the delicious undercurrent before managing to shake herself free.

Good Lord, Josie was right. She needed a holiday. But with her most recent business crisis breathing down her neck, sipping piña coladas beneath palm fronds wasn't likely any time soon. She'd take a holiday when she was back on her feet, when her business was back in the black. She wasn't about to give up on her dream.

She set the dog bed down and cleared the thickness from her throat. 'Rotties make great guard dogs as well as companions.'

On cue, the only male pup set his big front paws on the window; his tail whipped around back so hard, the motion almost knocked him over. Anyone who thought dogs didn't smile didn't know dogs.

She weaved around a giggling toddler, who clapped as Mr Cheese went hell-for-whiskers on his mouse wheel. 'He'll need walks. And puppy school to help socialise him.'

'Like kindergarten for dogs.' His arms crossed,

then he scratched his temple. 'How much time are we talking about? I get home late. I work most weekends too.'

Vanessa's heartbeat slowed. She should have guessed. His aura exuded energy and no-nonsense efficiency. Not that 'handsome high-powered executive' was a turn off. Just everyone seemed so busy these days—the twenty-first century treadmill gone mad. No one had time to walk their dogs and smell the flowers any more.

Her gaze flicked to his left hand—large, tanned but no gold ring. Still, not all those who were taken wore bands. As she'd found out.

'Perhaps your wife could help.'

'I'm not married.'

'Girlfriend?'

She was curious—only for the dog's sake. A workaholic man-god descended from warriors wouldn't be interested in an ordinary girl working her way up the ladder…lately one rung up, three rungs back.

'My housekeeper comes in once a week.'

She cut him a wry grin. *Not the same.*

She had a thought. 'If a dog's too much responsibility and a fish maybe isn't enough, perhaps a—'

'Don't say cat.' His chin and its deep cleft came down. 'I don't do cats.'

She almost rolled her eyes. What was it with men and moggies?

'A bird then? We have some lovely budgies. Or a

parrot? You can teach them to talk. Sit on your shoulder.'

The nostrils of his hawkish nose flared. 'I don't think so.'

She indicated a cage. 'What about a reptapet?'

'You mean a *snake*?' He visibly shuddered, a full body shiver. 'Pass.'

He skirted around an elderly man in a grey fedora squeaking at the guinea pigs to return to that tank and scrutinised the fish. Hovering above its yellow and blue bed stones, the fish blew a bubble and stared back. Looking closer, he lifted a hand to knock on the glass.

When she touched the platinum watch on his wrist—fish and tapping was a no-go zone—the fiery sensation of his skin on hers released a crackling zap hurtling up her limb. The scrumptious shockwave carried an arrow straight to her chest and stole the air from her lungs.

He straightened and looked at her oddly—a curious glint in his eye as if he might have felt the charge too. Or maybe that look simply said *hands off.*

Stepping back, she drew her tingling hand away. 'Plenty of people have satisfying relationships with fish,' she said in an unintentionally husky voice.

An intrigued smile swam in the depths of his eyes. 'Do you?'

Her glance took inventory of the wall of tanks behind them. 'We have scores of fish here.'

'But do you have fish at home?'

'No.'

'A dog?'

'I'm not allowed.'

His brows jumped. 'You live with your parents?'

She blinked twice. 'I rent.'

'But you have family close by.'

Her stomach lurched at his assumption. Orphaned at a young age, she'd been brought up by an aunt on the rural east coast of Australia. She had no brothers or sisters, grandparents or cousins. Other than Aunt McKenzie, she had no one.

She swallowed against a flush and regained control. 'I'm not sure that has anything to do with you buying a fish, Mr…'

'Stuart. Mitchell Stuart.' As if annoyed at himself, he waved a dismissive hand. 'And, no, it doesn't. *Totally* off track.' He narrowed his focus on the gaping fish again and slowly grinned. 'I think he'll do nicely.'

She forced her thoughts away from family—or lack thereof—and back onto business.

For a moment she'd wondered if this customer might enjoy a closer connection…someone to walk and have fun with. Guess she'd been mistaken.

But she was pleased for the fish; clearly he was going to a good home. She was sure he'd be fed the finest fish food and have his home regularly cleaned by the housekeeper.

She went to lift the tank. 'Do you have any names in mind?'

Frowning, Mr Stuart took over the weight of the tank. 'Fish have names?'

At the counter, she collected flakes, stabilising drops, a complimentary miniature Poseidon and his trident, then went through everything with Mr Stuart regarding the care of his new goldfish. After he'd scrawled a signature on the transaction slip, she handed back his card. 'I'm sure you'll have no problems.'

'If I do?'

'Call me.'

She whisked a business card from its holder. He gripped it, genuine victory shining in his eyes. 'I feel good about this.'

'Then so do I.'

Mr Stuart collected his bundles. On his way past the puppies, he faltered, but then shot a glance over his shoulder and held up the fish with a smile that said, Right decision.

She winked and saluted. Another satisfied customer. And the puppies would go quickly to homes filled with love and adequate attention. Maybe one day Mitchell Stuart would return when he was ready for a bigger commitment.

Would she still be here? She had to believe tomorrow's appointment with her bank manager would save the day. She couldn't bear to think of the alternative.

Two hours later, she flipped the sign on the door as the phone rang. If that was the feeders and drinkers supplier after a payment, the cheque was definitely in the mail. If it was the landlord reminding her to be out in two weeks...

She held her nervy stomach. Maybe she wouldn't answer.

When it rang again, she buckled and picked up. No hello from the other end, just a straight out, 'I've found a name for my fish.'

That deep voice was even more bone-melting over the phone—low and unconsciously inviting against her ear.

'Mr Stuart. Hello.'

'Kamikaze.'

She stammered. 'B-Beg your pardon?'

'He won't quit jumping out of the tank. He's on a suicide mission.'

She sank down onto a chair and rubbed her brow. Oh, dear. 'That sometimes happens.'

'I filled the tank, added the right amount of drops, set up the filter, gave him a feed. When I turned my back, he jumped out. I put him back in. He jumped out again, and again.' His voice dropped to a growl. 'Clearly he's not happy.'

'Could be a couple of things, like not enough water.'

'I've already put more in.'

'Maybe there's too much.'

His voice cracked. 'A fish can have too *much* water?'

'Only in so far as making it easier to leap out.' She gnawed her bottom lip. 'And then there's the possibility…'

'What possibility?'

'Some fish are just, well, *jumpers*.'

She heard his groan, then a shuffle as if he'd moved and dropped into a seat himself.

A vision flashed to mind: gorgeous Mitchell Stuart dead on his feet after staying up all night, a scoop in one hand, a fist made out of the other, ruing the day he'd ever set foot in Great and Small.

Vanessa gripped the receiver tight. She'd said she'd help if need be. Statistics said people bought pets from shops relatively close to their homes. Doctors made house calls. No reason she couldn't.

'Mr Stuart, I've just shut up shop. Would you like me to drop over and see what I can do?'

'You do that kind of thing?'

She lied. 'All the time.'

A relieved expulsion of air travelled down the line. 'I'll give you my address.'

'You think this is funny?' Mitch manoeuvred Kamikaze off his redwood dining table into the net and, suppressing a shudder, plopped him back into the tank water. 'Well, fun and games are *over*, buddy boy.'

Help was on the way. Help in the form of a petite, twenty-something-year-old whom he had no intention of getting to know beyond, *Thanks for saving my fish*. He wouldn't acknowledge Vanessa Craig's long, glossy hair, iridescent green eyes or the way his blood warmed like syrup on a stove whenever she smiled that *I'm totally harmless* smile. He was on sabbatical from women.

All women.

When his father had passed away fifteen years ago, Mitch had become the man of the house. Although he'd moved out of the stately Stuart mansion seven years ago, he was still the one the females of the family scampered to for help…and it seemed they *always* needed help. Help with their finances, help with repairs, booking flights, computer glitches—you name it, he got the call.

Like a stealthy airborne virus, recently the *helpless female factor* had followed him into more intimate relationships. Up-and-coming lingerie model Priscilla Lawson had seemed independent and resourceful when they'd met at that charity dinner. After three weeks together, their liaison had warmed up nicely, until Priscilla had tickled his chin one night and mentioned her family reunion… Would he mind booking her flight to Melbourne and, while she was gone, clean her pool and take her cat to its monthly check-up? It had liver problems.

His upper lip twitched.

He did *not* do cats.

But damn, he sure had liked that Rottweiler pup.

He was a busy man. His work was his life. However, while he had close associates at the firm as well as friends he knocked about with on weekends when he could spare the time, he'd wanted someone to come home to. Someone *male* who could watch football without a moan, not complain if he put his feet on the coffee table, who didn't flutter eyelashes or resort to tears to get their own way. Someone who didn't demand much time or emotion.

He gazed at his goggle-eyed companion.

A goldfish qualified.

The doorbell rang, echoing through the contemporary two-storey that enjoyed a privileged view of Sydney's magnificent harbour. Mitch rolled the tension from his shoulders, then stabbed a finger at Kami. 'Don't move a fin till I get back.'

He opened the door and there she stood, looking unaffected and fresh, one long leg pegged out in those bun-hugging jeans, conspicuously busty in her white T-shirt with the pink swirly logo that said *Great and Small*. If forced to vote, he would go with *Great* rather than *Small*. In fact, she looked pretty darn hot—

Mitch slammed on the mental brakes.

Sweet blazes, what was he doing? Visualising this woman naked wasn't going to help. In fact, it was highly inappropriate for more reasons than one.

Think 'fish', Mitch. Think 'through with females'.

Clearing his throat, he gestured her in. 'Thanks for coming so quickly. He's over here.'

In the dining room, Vanessa Craig set her hands on her knees and inspected the patient while Mitch stood back, eager for a diagnosis. When the examination went on and her left knee bent more, which meant her right hip hitched up, he scowled and scrubbed his jaw. If she'd done that on purpose, he didn't need the aggravation.

Finally she straightened, one hand on her lower back as she arched to stretch out her spine. Although *Great* jumped out at him, Mitch kept his eyes fixed firmly on hers.

Her question was sombre. 'When was the last time he jumped?'

'Just before you arrived.'

'Before that?'

'Ten minutes ago.'

Pensive, she stroked her chin. 'Could be he's still settling in.'

'Or tomorrow morning I could wake up and—'

Ack. He didn't want to think about it.

She crossed her arms. The letters *G* and *T* met at her cleavage. Not that he was looking. Same way he wasn't looking when she nibbled her lip and searched for an answer. Her mouth was naturally pink and very full. The highly kissable kind with delicate dimples on either side, as he'd already noted with some consternation earlier today.

'What if we try a bigger tank?' she suggested.

Mitch blinked back to the immediate problem. Increased volume equalled decreased risk, which added up to no dead fish in the morning. 'I like that plan.'

She moved towards the door. 'Good. I brought one with me. It's outside on your portico.'

Giving in to a smile, he followed. Clearly Vanessa Craig was intelligent, helpful, prompt as well as prepared. She was also a professional with her own business. Did her profit and loss sheets balance? Of course he was well aware *trouble* was not a gender specific trait. However, for too long now, it sure-as-Jack seemed that way.

He assisted Vanessa in with the larger tank and a few minutes later it was filled with the neutralising drops doing their work.

Hooking up the filter, she nodded almost shyly at the portrait on the wall. 'Is that your family?'

His chest constricted with a familiar sense of fondness tinged with regret. The photo featured his tall, lean father sitting on a red chaise longue surrounded by his wife, their four girls and only son.

His hand slid along the rim of the tank. 'My father passed away not long after that shot was taken.' Only days before Mitch's fifteenth birthday.

When she flicked on the filter, her hand accidentally brushed his. His heartbeat kicked as a live current spiralled up the cords of his arm to his shoulder, much the same heat-generating sensation that had claimed him this afternoon when they'd touched. Instantaneous and perilously pleasant.

Their eyes met—hers filled with perception as well as surprise before she dropped her gaze and edged a little away. 'I'm sorry…about your dad.'

Setting his thoughts straight, Mitch collected his trusty net. 'He was a good but old-fashioned man. A firm believer in tough love.'

Her mouth thinned. 'Spare the rod and spoil the child?'

'Not at all. But, in our house, actions had consequences.' How many talks about responsibility and putting those you cared about before yourself had he listened to? 'We were loved, but you didn't get away with much. In return, he gave us his undivided attention when we needed it.'

Her green eyes took on a sheen, reminding him of the leaves on the pavement this morning when he'd decided to get himself that pet.

'You must all miss him very much,' Vanessa said.

He nodded. *Every day.*

What would his father have done about the current family dilemma? Last night, Cynthia, the youngest at twenty-two, had announced her engagement to the sleaze ball of all time. Their showboating mother had crowed with joy, which had surprised him. Sleaze Ball might be a doctor but he was also a notorious gambler.

How on earth could he protect people who jumped feet first into disaster, tittering prettily as they fell into the abyss?

Groaning, he swirled the new water with the net.

Guess he'd sort something out. Or maybe he wouldn't; maybe this time would be the time he let the women sort it out themselves. He couldn't very well tell his sister who to marry, though he'd certainly like to tell her who *not* to.

Mitch stole a glance at his comely visitor as a gentle reflection from the water danced over her face. Did Vanessa Craig hold high expectations on the business front, or was she focused more on personal matters, like landing a good catch? Seemed his sisters could think of little other than having babies. What was the hurry? He was in no hurry at all.

He set the net down. 'What about you?'

Her bright eyes blinked up from the water. 'What about me?'

'Family. You didn't say whether yours live nearby.'

Her slender shoulders went up, then down. 'I don't have a family.'

None? The idea was alien. And, in some ways, wickedly appealing. No demands. No expectations. No interruptions. 'No one at all?'

She trailed a damp hand down her jeans, leaving a streak on her shapely denim thigh. 'I have an aunt. As well as great friends and my animals—' she flashed an optimist's smile '—so life's full.'

Was that a subtle hint that she wasn't interested in romance? Well, ditto…even if his growing curiosity and flexing libido refuted that statement. There was something about Vanessa Craig—something mesmerising calling to him from beyond those bewitching green eyes.

She checked her large-faced watch, took the net and scooped Kami up to ease him into his new watery home. As his golden scales darted around the relocated trident, Mitch shot out a relieved breath. 'He looks happier already.'

'Hopefully that should do the trick.'

'After all that exercise, he should sleep well.' Which was good news for them both; he had some important paperwork to get through tonight.

'Fish don't sleep,' she pointed out. 'They slow their metabolism and rest.' She knelt down to gather the replacement tank's packaging. 'Dolphins sleep, of course,' she went on. 'But they're mammals. They keep one side of their brain awake while the other half dozes.'

Fascinated, he dropped onto his haunches too. He'd known dolphins weren't fish, but, 'They're awake while they sleep?'

Clearly he was behind in his general knowledge. Maybe he should subscribe to the Animal channel. Or he could cut his more primal instincts some slack and become better acquainted with this expert. Not as if he was taking the plunge and asking her out. He was simply interested in getting to know her mind a little better.

He collected some discarded bubble wrap. 'Did you study marine biology?'

'Zoology. And business as well as some Greek mythology.' Sweeping up more packaging, she tilted her head at him and shimmering hair fell like a silky waterfall from behind her shoulder. 'Did you know that the ancient Greeks believed dolphins were once human? There's a school of thought that says Poseidon was human once too.'

Still crouching, he leant a little closer. The sound of her voice was melodic…soothing. 'Is that right?'

'The more traditional myth says he was one of the supreme Olympian gods,' she continued, grabbing more packaging. 'When Creation was divided between the gods, Hades got to rule the underworld, Zeus dominated the skies, and Poseidon became lord of the water, both fresh and salt. His son, Triton, was half human, half fish.'

Engrossed, Mitch blindly reached for more bubble wrap while she reached the same way. Their hands touched. That sizzle flashed again and this time sparked and caught light. But while the sexual awareness was through the roof, the sense of awkwardness had all but vanished.

They shared a brief *what if* smile, then she pushed to her feet.

He wanted to hear more. 'So the mermaid legend started with the Greeks?'

She nodded. 'But originally mermaids were called sirens, fabled to be half woman, half bird. They had beautiful voices they used to lure sailors and their ships onto the rocks. If a ship got away, the siren would have to throw herself into the sea.'

He slowly pushed to his feet too, chancing to take in the tempting lines of her body as he went. Vanessa Craig didn't smell like birdseed or puppies any more. She smelled soft, sweet and slightly salty, like a fresh ocean breeze.

He rested his hip against the table edge. 'Did any sailors try to resist?'

'One. He'd heard about the sirens hypnotic deadly powers. He had his crew tie him to the mast of his ship so he wasn't able to steer her towards tragedy. But when he saw the beautiful siren on the shore, and heard her song, he begged to be cut free.'

His gaze skimmed her delicate jaw. 'Who won?'

She laughed. 'Depends if you were the siren or the sailor.'

His return smile faded as his gaze drifted to her mouth. Those pink, full, tempting lips. Another few inches and he could taste them. Explore them. Of course this instant attraction could merely be backlash from shunning the dating scene long enough. Vanessa was attractive, intelligent, not to mention incredibly sexy.

Best of all, she was independently minded. A strong but companionable woman. *His* kind of woman.

He broke the trance and bent to sweep the box off the floor. 'Have you had your business long?'

'Two years.'

'Going well?'

Her smile wavered and she shrugged. 'Sure. Aside from being evicted in two weeks from the store I adore and needing to find a new place with rent that's anywhere within my budget. I have an appointment with my bank manager tomorrow and—' She stopped and released a self-deprecating sigh. 'Now *that* was too much information.'

His gut turned to ice as a withering feeling sank through his middle, but Mitch managed a thin smile in return. 'Not too much information at all.'

Rather, just enough. Barring an earthquake in central Sydney or the acting President suddenly losing all faith in his protégé, two weeks from tomorrow Mitch would claim the head chair of the family company, as per his late father's will. If anyone could organise finance, the soon-to-be

President of Stuart Investments and Loans certainly could.

But, realistically, he and Vanessa Craig were little more than acquaintances. Despite the lure of smouldering embers, he wouldn't ignore the warning signs. Eviction. Financial disaster. Before him stood a time bomb about to explode, which translated into a loss for his company should he choose to invest, not to mention a hit to his personal armoury if he allowed himself to become any more intrigued. God knew, he had enough to worry about without taking on new risks.

He held the box against his ribs and glanced around. 'Well, that seems to be it,' he announced cheerily. 'How much do I owe you?'

Reading his terminating social cue, her smile wavered and her gaze flicked away. 'No charge.'

'There must be some difference between the two tanks.'

'All part of the service.' She nodded at her card on the table. 'And if you need any help in the next few days, you know where to find—'

'Absolutely.' He snatched up the card with his free hand as if to confirm his commitment. 'I'll see you out.'

A moment later, he swung open his front door and faced the sunset's dying colours, deepest crimson and streaks of gold bleeding across the eucalypt hills in the west.

'Goodnight, Mr Stuart.' She gave him her signature salute. 'Good luck.'

'Yep. Thanks. You too.'

She'd need it.

When the door closed, he emptied his lungs, tossed her business card on the hallstand and made a vow. If he had any more problems with Kami, he'd call a fish expert; *Yellow Pages* were bound to list them. The best way not to get burned was to stay away from the fire, no matter how attractive the flames of that fire might be.

But as he strode towards the living room, a tantalising image swam up to taunt him…those heavenly hips, that amazing T-shirt, her hypnotic voice and come-hither smile.

Damp broke out on his hairline and he wheeled back around. Grabbing the card, he looked at it hard and tore it clean down the middle.

Beautiful sirens. Sailors sinking with their ships. The only rocks he wanted to see were the ones clinking in his pre-dinner Scotch while he pored over those figures for tomorrow's late meeting.

He settled down to that drink and his work, with the new tank and its occupant on a side table nearby. He was trying to banish Vanessa Craig and her lips to the furthermost corners of his mind when the doorbell rang.

He slammed down his glass. *What now?*

A moment later he swung open the door and his heart hit his throat.

'Me again.' An apologetic but upbeat Vanessa Craig curled some hair behind her ear. 'I got down the street before realising I forgot to collect the smaller tank. I bet you don't want it clogging up your gorgeous home—'

Her words ran dry at the same time her face fell.

Her gaze had drifted behind him, to the hallstand at his back.

To the torn business card.

As his insides wrenched into a guilty knot, she blinked several times, then her mouth quivered with a lame smile—a vain attempt to cover her hurt. 'Gee, I didn't realise I'd made such a sterling impression.'

He ran a hand through his hair. *Hell.*

'It's not how it looks.'

Her laugh was short. 'It looks like you can't bear to see my name.'

He groaned. She had it completely wrong, but he couldn't tell her that. He couldn't begin to explain.

Her chin angled up. 'Whatever your opinion of my service today, you're one hundred per cent entitled to it. The customer's always right. Always.' She forced a brave smile, then turned on her heel.

'Even when the customer screws up,' he said, 'because he's attracted to the lady in charge?'

She turned back, her jaw hanging. 'What did you say?'

He gripped both sides of the door jamb and admitted what must be obvious. 'I'm attracted to you.'

She shook her head, puzzled. 'So you don't want to contact me again?'

She was right. His reasoning was flawed, particularly now she was back, with her lips so near and his elevated testosterone levels demanding to know what the hell he was waiting for.

He held his breath.

What *was* he waiting for?

His hands left the jamb and found her upper arms. Drawing her close—with that maddening logo pressed against his chest—he dropped his mouth over hers.

Her body stiffened and her fists came up, two small rocks pushing against his collarbone. But he didn't release her…truth tell, he couldn't. The heat combusting between their bodies had fused them together; she was glued to him as much as he was to her.

As his mouth opened, her lips parted and the kiss evolved and deepened, growing beyond spur-of-the-moment into something-special. His hold on her arms eased; as if a crutch were removed, she leant against his length. Taking the cue, his tongue performed a lazy sweep against hers, and again. Her relaxed fists began kneading his shirt.

When a compliant mew vibrated in her throat, he imagined slipping that T-shirt over her head and running his hands over the sweetest heaven on earth. His blood felt on fire. Every red-hot ion ready to ignite. God help him, he didn't want to stop.

The kiss broke gradually, reluctantly, the caress growing strong again before, hot lava flowing through his veins, he finally eased off.

Her eyes were closed, her breathing ragged. Out of breath himself, he murmured against her warm soft lips, 'Now do you see?'

Her eyelids flickered and her focus sharpened. 'You wanted to *kiss* me?'

'Very much.'

'And you thought I wouldn't want you to?'

Wincing, he pulled slightly back. 'That's not quite it.'

Her shoulders sank. 'Is it another woman?'

He groaned to himself. 'Not just one.'

When she unravelled herself from what remained of his grasp, he rubbed his brow. How could he explain that he didn't need any more ties?

'What I mean is, sexual attraction is one thing, but compatibility should be built on—' He stopped, then started again. 'When two people get together, they should be on the same page as far as—' No, that wasn't right. He took a breath. 'Well, the thing is—'

'That water should meet its own level?' She darted a wounded glance towards his spacious living room and, beyond that, the priceless view. 'Is that what you're trying to say?'

He exhaled. 'I'm saying we don't know each other very well.'

'But you know enough.'

'Vanessa—'

As he stepped forward, she stepped back and held up a hand. 'Please don't be embarrassed. I'm a pragmatist, Mr Stuart. I know the way the world works.' She reached around and took her torn card from the hallstand. 'In case you're tempted.'

With infuriating good grace, she shut the door behind her. It took all his willpower not to call out and drag her back against him where she seemed to belong. He *had* wanted to kiss her, hold her… Damn it, in that moment of insanity, he'd wanted to peel the clothes from her body and make love to her, thoroughly and all night long.

But, as he'd said, he barely knew this woman and his rescuing-damsels-in-distress plate was full. He shouldn't get involved. In fact, he should thank his lucky stars it was over before it had begun.

He strode to the wet bar and poured himself a fresh Scotch. He swallowed a gulp, swallowed another. Frustration winning out, he smashed the glass down on the counter.

Like it or not, he was *already* involved. He wanted to see Vanessa Craig again. He wanted to listen to her stories. Taste her sweet lips. Damn it, he wanted to *help*.

The six million dollar question was…

CHAPTER TWO

How do I get myself out of this mess?

The following afternoon, Vanessa sat on the top tier of the Opera House steps. Squawking seagulls wheeled overhead while chattering tourists and other visitors swirled all around, many gazing up to marvel at the giant shells.

The construction of the Opera House had taken seventeen years to build. The end result was extraordinary in aesthetic, acoustic as well as patriotic terms. Whenever Vanessa needed to find strength and inspiration, she came here to appreciate what could be accomplished if one only tried.

Now she looked out over the water, busy with Sydney's commuter ferries, past the bridge's magnificent glinting steel arch and into the haze of her unknown future.

From the age of ten—the year she'd realised her parents really weren't coming back to collect her from Aunt McKenzie's—her heart had been set on finding homes for others. That was what made her

happy. What kept her connected. Without her store—
her *purpose*—she'd feel…

She gazed at the seagulls.

Adrift.

Her cellphone vibrated in her trouser suit pocket. The darkening line of the horizon smudged as
she put the phone to her ear. 'Great and Small.
Vanessa speaking.'

'Oh, I'm *tho* glad to have caught you.'

Vanessa flipped through her mental PDA. An
elderly woman, enthusiastic, with a slight lisp didn't
ring a bell. Another creditor after a payment?

She suppressed a worn-down sigh. 'Yes, this is
she. How can I help?'

'My son, Mitchell, gave me your number. He said
you were the lady I needed to see.' Her voice
lowered. 'He altho mentioned you do house calls.'

Vanessa straightened from her slouch. Mitchell
Stuart, aka Mr Goldfish?

At one stage, when she and Mitch Stuart had
spoken about sirens, she'd felt increasingly drawn to
him. He'd looked at her with those startling blue eyes
and her nerve-endings had reached out and tingled.
Then his expression had dropped from simmering to
a degree below tepid and she'd known why.

She'd shared personal information regarding her
financial situation with a veritable stranger. She'd
come across as needy…perhaps even soliciting. Her
upbringing had been humble and she'd been raised to
value tenacity and dignity; she should've known better.

God, she should never have returned to get the smaller tank. Worse, she shouldn't have allowed him to kiss her as she'd never been kissed before. Though it was clear they'd both enjoyed the interaction, that wasn't enough. She'd read him right when he'd first walked into her shop.

Water meets its own level. Guys like him—guys with money and family and the world at their feet—didn't end up with girls like her. But she couldn't very well hang up on his mother.

She quietly released that pent-up breath. 'What can I do for you, Mrs Stuart?'

'Cockapoos.'

'Also known as spoodles,' she confirmed. Cocker spaniels mixed with poodles.

'In the past I've always purchased toy poodles.'

Vanessa remembered. The little yappy ones. Was Mrs Stuart in the market for a puppy? 'I don't have any cockapoos in store at the moment.'

'My son regards your expertise highly. He said you'd be able to help. I'm after four as soon as possible. I'm willing to pay for the best.'

Vanessa's toes curled as she squeezed the phone tight. The bank representative she'd spoken with late this afternoon had turned her application for a loan down flat. His exact words: *it's best to face reality, cut your losses and find a paying job.* But pedigree cockapoos sold for a great deal. If she tracked down and sold four, the extra funds could keep the wolf from the door, perhaps long enough to find a way to keep Great and Small alive and in its current location.

If there was any way, she wanted to stay where she was. The shop was set up exactly how she'd always envisaged. It was far more than a business.

It was her home.

'Miss Craig? Are you there?'

Vanessa pushed to her feet. 'How soon do you want them?'

'The sooner the better.'

She was already jogging down the steps, phone still pressed to her ear. 'I'll make some enquiries and call you back.'

'I'd prefer if you'd drop by.'

To pass on a few details? She didn't see the point. But Mrs Stuart did indeed sound pampered and Vanessa wasn't in a position to argue.

The customer was always right, particularly one with a few thousand to spend. She should be grateful Mitch Stuart was man enough to let bygones be bygones. He'd forgiven—and most likely forgotten—their embarrassing moment and had put his mother's needs before any hard feelings. She, in turn, would be professional and do her best to track down those dogs.

Thirty minutes and three phone calls later, Vanessa turned her Honda CRV into the address Mrs Stuart had provided. A mansion greeted her, its stately sandstone walls surrounded by immaculate mint-green lawns. A Union Jack and Southern Cross flag, perched atop a mast that touched the sky, flapped in the cool early evening breeze.

She'd thought Mitch's stylish contemporary abode was something special, but this place might have belonged to royalty. She remembered her own single bedroom granny flat and mismatched furniture and sighed. His world and hers were not only miles apart—they were light years.

After parking on the paved circular drive, she swallowed her jangle of nerves, ascended the stone steps and rang the bell that droned a sombre tune behind the imposing ten-foot-high oak door. A uniformed maid, with a severe overbite that reminded Vanessa of Mr Cheese, answered the door. Before either of them could speak, Mrs Stuart scurried across the polished timber floor and into view.

'Come in, come in.' Mrs Stuart waved Vanessa in, then called over her butter-yellow blouse shoulder, 'Cynthia! The dog lady's here.'

Vanessa cringed. Had Mitch suggested she call her that?

Mrs Stuart addressed the maid. 'Thank you, Wendle. I'll take care of our guest.'

Wendle left them and Mrs Stuart linked her arm through Vanessa's, guiding her down a wide hall trimmed in ornate dark timber, into an elaborately furnished living room—decorative high ceiling, polished brass and crystal fittings, baroque couches and window seats pulled from the pages of *Celebrity House and Garden*.

On the far couch, a woman around Vanessa's age lifted her reddened nose from a lace handkerchief. She was finely boned and, although unwashed, her hair looked blonde like her mother's. However, rather than hazel, her eyes were ocean-blue like her brother's, and rimmed with red.

Cynthia found the strength to mutter, 'Nice to meet you.'

Mrs Stuart clasped her bejewelled hands under her chin. Diamonds and rubies flashed in the dying sunlight slanting in through a tall arched window. 'Our Cynthia has had a bad time of it. Day before yesterday she was engaged. Today, sadly, she is not.'

Vanessa cocked a brow. These people mightn't mind laying open their private lives in the parlour but, after yesterday's blabbermouth experience with Mitch Stuart, she'd learned her lesson. She wouldn't divulge the fact that she'd once lived through a similar ordeal.

She'd once dated a good-looking man of some means. He'd been charming, but something beyond mysterious about him had sent up a red flag. When, after two months, she'd suggested they have a break, he'd vowed he couldn't give her up, then he'd popped the question. She'd been flattered but unconvinced. Good thing she hadn't made a fool of herself and accepted, because the following day she'd received a call: apparently he was already engaged to someone more befitting his station. The ruffled female caller with the superior tone had said Vanessa was his 'fluff on the side'.

At least animals didn't omit the truth or flat out lie. What you saw was what you got.

'I'm sorry about your news,' Vanessa said sincerely. Then, squaring her shoulders, she moved forward with business. 'You were interested in acquiring four cockapoos?'

Mrs Stuart sat beside her daughter and patted her hand. 'Cynthia looked into purchasing one before…well, before this terrible affair. I thought going ahead and finding her a little friend would help. Then I got to thinking. My darling Sheba passed away six months ago.'

The calculation wasn't difficult. 'That's only two puppies.'

'Two each makes four,' Mrs Stuart corrected. 'It's nice for them to have company. Cynthia and an older sister live in the cottage on the adjoining lot, so it'd be a real little family.'

Vanessa's heart warmed. She would've loved to have had a brother or sister growing up…Christmases, birthdays, boisterous family Sunday dinners. Maybe one day—if she was lucky.

'I've made a couple of phone calls,' she said, happy to proceed. Dogs were great company at any time, particularly when someone needed a friend who didn't judge and always listened. And more than instinct said any puppy sold to these women would certainly be cared for. 'A litter sired by a world champion should be available this week. Is that too soon?'

Mrs Stuart squeezed her daughter's free hand. 'I

should think the sooner the better.' The older woman's gaze drifted to the left and her face lit up. 'Mitch, darling. Your friend's arrived.'

Vanessa's blood pressure dropped and the room tilted forty-five degrees.

Good Lord, she hadn't known *he'd* be here.

She wheeled around to see Mitch Stuart sauntering into the room. His languid yet purposeful gait was that of a man effortlessly in charge. His smile was just as sexy, even if the slant of his lips was a little contrite. Vanessa's stomach muscles tugged. She wanted to run—from this house or straight into those strong arms? She wasn't certain which.

Warning herself not to, Vanessa nonetheless breathed in the subtle male scent as he stopped beside her. He was taller than she remembered, his shoulders in that crisp white Oxford shirt, sleeves rolled below the elbows, seemed far broader. His eyes were so blue and filled with light, she imagined she saw herself in their reflection.

He spoke to his mother but kept his eyes on their guest. 'Miss Craig and I are acquaintances, Mother.'

'Then your *acquaintance* is helping us no end,' Mrs Stuart replied. 'Vanessa thinks we can have our puppies by the end of the week.'

His chest inflated as that smile grew and simmered in his eyes. 'That's great news.'

Vanessa wondered…

He'd ripped up her business card, had kissed her passionately, then as good as admitted he didn't want to get involved, which was far nobler than stringing her along. Was this meeting about salving his conscience as much as helping his mother and sister? If that were the case, she would be wise to accept his peace offering graciously. Aunt McKenzie had often warned against false pride.

She'd be grateful but, foremost, businesslike.

Vanessa allowed a crisp smile. 'Thanks for the referral.'

'Least I could do.'

Had he stepped closer or was it that seductive rich tone pulling at her again?

Determined to ignore the rapid heartbeat thudding in her ears, Vanessa tucked in her chin. She needed to move this along. They'd already established that, whatever it was bubbling between herself and Mitch Stuart, it was going nowhere fast.

She faced Mrs Stuart. 'Would you mind if I had a look at the dogs' accommodation?'

She'd like to pass on any positive information to the breeders. Plus her enquiry would get her out of the room and away from the temptation of Mitch Stuart's hypnotic presence. She was human, after all.

Preoccupied, Cynthia sniffed, dropped the handkerchief to her lap and shuddered. Her mother clucked comfortingly and looked to her son. 'Mitch, can you show Vanessa Sheba's housing for me?'

Vanessa felt her eyes widen. She hadn't meant for Mitch to take her on a tour. She should've kept quiet.

Of course, he could always decline.

But his smile was dazzling. 'My pleasure. Follow me.' He tipped his head towards the ornate arch through which he'd entered the room.

Vanessa found her calm centre and braced herself. She could handle this. She was a mature, intelligent woman with a goal. She could spend a few moments alone with Mitch Man-god Stuart. She was hardly in danger of him kissing her again, particularly here, in his mother's home. They'd established he didn't want to get involved—they weren't 'compatible'.

It was her imagination, then, that something almost predatory gleaming in his eyes whispered otherwise.

He matched his stride with hers and they passed a sitting room, what looked like a study, then a massive library, boasting book spines to the ceiling. The very walls seemed to breathe an extended family history of privilege.

He swung a left. Given the increasingly delicious aroma, she guessed they were approaching the kitchen.

He surprised her with his question. 'How did your bank meeting go today?'

She took a moment to find a casual tone. 'No need to try to make conversation, Mr Stuart.'

'No good, huh?'

She pressed her lips together and looked straight ahead.

'I'd like to help.'

She sent him a questioning look. 'By sending more business my way?'

Did he have a swag of friends after companions? Not that that would be a long-term solution.

'I was thinking more along the lines of a loan.'

Vanessa stopped dead and measured the earnest expression in his eyes. Well, that was out of the blue. Just what was behind that offer? Surely he wasn't in the habit of gifting money to women he barely knew. Just what did he expect in exchange?

She set off walking again and they entered a huge kitchen. 'Thanks, but I don't take money from strangers.'

'Acquaintance, remember? And I run an invest-ment and lending organisation. Helping with finance is what I do.'

She digested the information and slid him a jaded smile. 'You've suddenly decided to throw me a line?' Odd that he'd neglected to mention his profession last night, and he'd certainly had the ideal opportunity.

'We'd known each other five minutes. I've had time to think it over.'

'Think over being charitable or kissing me and wishing you hadn't?'

When his brows shot up, she walked a little faster.

She hadn't meant to be that blunt, but she wasn't in the mood for games, not where her beloved shop was concerned. And all these shining pans hanging from their gleaming hooks, the sparkling sinks set in glistening granite benches… This environment was so overly advantaged, goose bumps were erupting up and down her limbs. She'd see the dogs' housing, then get out of here fast, back to her own safe little world where she belonged.

He scratched his temple. 'You're not going to make this easy for me, are you?'

A perfect retort burned on the tip of her tongue. But she thought again and swallowed the words.

Annoying thing was that she had nothing to lose and everything to gain by putting their sizzling mistake of an embrace behind her, as he had clearly done. She needed a loan. He'd offered professional help. So he'd kissed her and didn't want to go there again. So what? She'd lived through worse and survived.

She pulled up by the million-dollar coffee machine and folded her arms. 'What would you like to know?'

Long legs braced shoulder-width apart, he mimicked her no-nonsense pose. 'Firstly, what are you seeking to gain out of your business?'

Puzzled, she shook her head. 'What do you mean?'

'Do you envisage yourself as a multimillionaire? Is it a living you fell into? Something to keep you out of trouble or a passion? Today's business world is more competitive than ever, as you've no doubt found out. A person can lose everything. The veritable shirt off his back.'

Wow. What an optimist.

If she'd clung to every negative piece of advice she'd been handed in her life, she mightn't get out of bed in the morning.

'I'm aware of life's knocks. Doesn't mean I don't

deserve my chance to provide the community with a service which I believe in, heart and soul.'

He studied her eyes for a calculating moment, then a grin kicked up a corner of his mouth and his arms unravelled. 'All right, then. Let's go through the figures, work on a business plan and we can take it from there.'

'I already have a business plan.'

'Obviously not a good one.'

Guess she had to give him that. She liked to consider herself independent; she'd done everything on her own, making mistakes and learning along the way. Not quickly enough, it seemed.

He set off again and she followed him into an adjoining room that might have been set up for infants— pastel pinks and blues, pint-sized cushiony beds, a playground with colourful balls and squeezy toys. Lucky dogs. But, before she commented on the quality accommodation, she wanted to push home a point.

'I appreciate your interest in my situation. But I want to make it clear that I'm not a charity case.' In other words, 'I don't want you to consider approving a loan simply because…' *Say it, Vanessa. Just say it.* 'Because you feel bad about last night.'

A muscle in his shadowed jaw flexed as he faced her. His subtle scent and aura of strength soaked into her skin, ambushing a good measure of her bravado and turning it to mush.

'While we're on the subject of getting things straight…I don't regret kissing you, Vanessa. Quite the contrary.' That curious gleam flared up and swam again in his eyes. 'Would it surprise you to hear I'd like to do it again?'

A hot jet of arousal flashed through her veins. For a moment, she was so shaken she couldn't respond. She wet her suddenly dry lips, then wished she hadn't. She didn't want to give him the wrong idea.

Her voice was a croak. 'That wouldn't be wise.'

The line between his brows gradually deepened. 'You're right. Of course. Not wise at all.'

'Clearly you have misgivings about me…*you* and me. *Us.* If we're going to be associated in a business sense, it wouldn't be appropriate to be…involved.'

Yet she melted as his head tipped, he focused on her lips and stepped closer. 'I agree. Totally.'

Her face grew tellingly warm, her legs frighteningly weak. 'It could cause problems.'

His fingertip lightly curved her cheek, around her chin, sending wondrous warmth unfurling through her system. 'I don't need any more problems.'

He gently pinched her chin, tipping her face a fraction higher, and a lightning bolt zapped and sizzled from her crown down to her toes. 'Me either.' Definitely not.

With his gaze scalding her lips, he moved unbearably close, until his hard lean hips met hers. 'So it's settled.'

She sighed and murmured, 'Absolutely.'

His lips touched hers and gently lingered, tasting, enjoying, until her fluttering soul grew wings and carried her away. When he carefully drew back, her senses were reeling and her feet no longer touched the ground.

She gazed up dreamily, lost in the entrancing mirrors of his eyes. 'So was that just part of the service?'

His jaw tightened. 'No. That was unforgivable. It won't happen again.'

'You're certain?'

The pad of his thumb grazed her lips before his mouth descended once more. 'Absolutely.'

CHAPTER THREE

AS THEY came up for air, Vanessa sensed something at her back. A prickling. A stare. Then Mitch's smouldering eyes left hers, he straightened and cleared his throat.

'Mother. We didn't hear you come in.'

Vanessa swung around. Mrs Stuart's smile was easy. Almost too easy.

'I don't mean to interrupt,' the older woman apologised.

Vanessa absently finger combed her hair and shot a glance over her surroundings. For a moment, she'd forgotten where she was, which happened to be *way out of her depth*.

'We were just...er...looking around,' Vanessa mumbled.

Mrs Stuart moved forward. 'And you're happy with the accommodation?'

'I'm sure your dogs won't want for a thing.'

Delighted, Mrs Stuart clasped her hands and her smile grew. 'Then we'd best get this arrangement underway. Mitch, I've written a cheque for a goodwill deposit. It's on the credenza in the living room. Vanessa and I will be right behind you. I want to ask her something…about the puppies.'

Mitch gave a hesitant half grin, but he inhaled and nodded as if it wasn't worth the argument. 'I'll see you both soon.'

Before Mitch left the room, he sent Vanessa a secret wink. Heartbeat skipping, she winked back. Her return gesture was almost involuntary, like accepting his kiss a moment ago. Before Mitch, she hadn't come close to understanding the true meaning of the word *magnetism*.

Both women's gazes followed his retreat, Vanessa's sculpting over the wide rolling shoulders, trim waist, lean hips and long, strong legs.

'My son's a good-looking man.'

Vanessa acknowledged the obvious. 'He is that.'

They began to walk, Mrs Stuart's hands still clasped at her waist. 'He'll be a wonderful catch for any woman.'

Vanessa's step faltered and she slid a curious gaze Mrs Stuart's way. 'I don't want to leave you with the wrong idea. Mitch and I have only just met.' A kiss or two was hardly death us do part.

'Ah, but the seeds are quickly blossoming into romance.' Mrs Stuart's laugh was light. 'My dear, a blind man could see.'

Vanessa's cheeks toasted. How could she deny it? 'There are…certain feelings.'

They moved through the kitchen, Mrs Stuart

nodding at Wendle, who was busy rotating roast potatoes. When they were out of household staff earshot, Mrs Stuart stated, 'You're not a virgin, are you, dear.'

Vanessa choked out a strangled cough. 'I beg your pardon?' Mrs Stuart might like to be open, but this was taking freedom of information way too far.

'It's no secret my son is drawn to women of… well…*experience*.'

Even if it were broadcast on *Entertainment Tonight*, Vanessa didn't feel right discussing Mitch's love life with his mother, of all people. Although now, truth tell, she was a smidgeon curious.

And what, precisely, constituted *experience*? She'd had more than one lover; last time she heard that didn't translate into promiscuous.

As they passed the solemn library, the musty air seemed to wind out and smother her as Mrs Stuart's heels on the timber clacked and echoed dully through the hall.

'Please don't take advantage of him.'

Vanessa lost her breath at the same time her back went up. 'How on earth would I do that?'

Mrs Stuart raised a brow. 'A woman from your quarter has her means.'

As they moved into the living room, Mitch joined them. Her brain stuck on freeze-frame, Vanessa automatically accepted the cheque he offered. She barely registered the generous amount penned above Mrs Stuart's neat signature.

Mrs Stuart's smile was staid. 'I'm sure it'll be very pleasant doing business with you.'

Business, sure. But Mrs Stuart wasn't about to dance at Vanessa's wedding, particularly if it was to her son. Which wasn't on the cards. Not even close. Stock from different pots rarely blended. It might be the twenty-first century but, at its deepest level, class structure was still alive and well. If the torn card last night had been an indication, Mrs Stuart's performance today proved it.

So what did all that mean for today's kiss? And Mitch's let's-take-this-further wink?

Mitch's rich tone seeped in through the fog. 'We'll leave you and Cynthia to your meal, Mother.'

Mrs Stuart's face fell. 'Oh, Mitch. Won't you stay for dinner?'

'Not tonight.' He stooped and brushed a kiss on her cheek.

Mrs Stuart pouted. 'I'm disappointed.'

'Next time.' He took Vanessa's elbow. 'Vanessa and I have some things to discuss.'

Mrs Stuart's mouth pinched before a flawless smile covered it. 'Then I'll say goodnight.'

The lady of the house didn't accompany them out. As the door closed and they descended the stone steps into the twilight, Vanessa shivered at the chill creeping up her spine.

Mitch stopped, concerned. 'What's wrong?'

She bit her lip. Should she tell him about her conversation with Mrs Stuart? She had no hands-on experience with mothers; her aunt had been a good provider and wonderfully supportive when crunch time rolled around. Were mothers supposed to wedge themselves into their children's lives this way under the guise of protectiveness? She suspected not.

She stole a glance at the imposing front door. Still shut. A ruffle of the curtain was no doubt her imagination.

She'd left that house with Mrs Stuart holding the upper hand. But she couldn't take another step without being honest with Mitch.

'I think your mother just warned me not to seduce you.'

To say it aloud sounded absurd. But Mitch merely grinned.

Vanessa narrowed her eyes. 'You're not surprised?'

They continued to walk to her car. 'My mother doesn't approve of any woman I see. They're either too vain, too thin, too haughty, too extrovert.' He gave a wry grin. 'I could go on.'

How about too poor?

Although Mrs Stuart's observations weren't personal, her comments were no less hurtful. 'She sounds difficult to please.'

'On that level, impossible. My mother's a widow's widow, with a stake in maintaining the status quo.'

As he opened her car door, Vanessa put the pieces together. 'You're single. She and her daughters are your only family.'

'She misses my father a great deal.' He left the obvious unsaid: his mother relied on him far too much.

She'd taken umbrage at Mrs Stuart's questioning, but now Vanessa succumbed to a twinge of sympathy. It was horrible to lose those you loved and depended on; she couldn't remember her parents but she missed them every day and to the deepest level of her being. What if she were to find the love of her life, only to have him taken away? She wouldn't be able to bear it.

Forearm resting on the open door rim, he peered in. 'Now, what say we get this plan underway?'

Vanessa's mind flew back to the critical here and now. 'Our business plan?' She checked her watch. 'But it's getting late.'

He frowned. 'Vanessa, we need to dive into this as soon as possible. How about we meet at your shop?'

Josie had looked after the shop this afternoon so Vanessa could keep her appointment with the bank. She shook her head. 'The animals will be settled for the night.' The dogs and kittens were bedded down at the local vet each night, but Vanessa didn't like to disturb the others.

'Your house, then.'

After seeing the pristine existence Mitch had grown up in, God, no! He'd liken her granny flat to a slum.

She made a flippant excuse. 'It's a mess.'

One big shoulder pushed to his ear. 'Then it has to be my place.'

Still no good. After that last kiss, there was only

one place 'close proximity' could lead and it wasn't to Grandma's house.

She may not be anywhere near as experienced as Mrs Stuart would like to believe. However, she was in tune with her sexuality: she was attracted to Mitch and, as he'd made clear again a moment ago, he was attracted to her. But, as they'd both already stated— none too convincingly—it wasn't wise to mix rags with riches, or business with pleasure.

Last year, Josie had bowed to temptation and slept with her boss at the accounting firm she'd worked for. When his superior had found out, he'd assigned Josie to a different branch. It'd taken boss man three weeks to start up an affair with his new assistant.

And there was another concern. If she and Mitch did end up acting on this sexual buzz and sleeping together, wouldn't that make any acceptance of a loan feel more like some kind of payment? What if 'good times' turned bad and he decided to wield his power and pull the loan? Then she *would* be screwed. Vanessa liked to be optimistic, not careless.

'Do you like Chinese food?' he asked.

She blinked and answered instinctively. 'I do.' Chow mein was her favourite.

'I'll order in.' He flashed that killer smile. 'You know the address. I'll see you in, say, an hour.'

As he moved to close the door, panic hit Vanessa like a medicine ball to the stomach. This was happening too fast. She just wasn't sure.

'*Wait.*'

He swung the door back open. His expression was accommodating, but with a sultry hint of *I'm hungry in more ways than one*.

Her hands wrung the steering wheel as she nibbled her lip.

In or out. Yes or no. Chicken or go-for-it.

Finally she released a breath and offered a yielding smile. 'Don't forget the fortune cookies.'

He pulled up straight, unintentionally emphasizing that dynamite chest. 'Will do.'

He closed the door and walked towards the black sports car parked to the side of the drive. Vanessa watched his retreat in the side mirror, her mouth becoming progressively drier.

So commanding and refined; he couldn't guess that she talked to rodents and reptiles and sometimes wondered if they talked back. Or that her favourite dessert was pink jellybean smiley faces on caramel swirl ice cream. That should be enough to put anyone off, particularly when they were routinely served crème brûlée with a solid-gold spoon.

Setting her jaw, she fired the ignition and pumped the pedal. This—*them*—whatever the combustible emotion she was feeling—wasn't meant to be. Not even for one unforgettable, orgasm-filled night. There was too much that didn't fit.

Too much at stake.

When she got home she'd call; she had his number listed on the receipt info. She'd explain that she'd developed a headache and it would be best she made a time to see him at his office. Should he deem her little enterprise worthy of the chance, she'd say thank you for the loan, then leave well enough alone.

No way, no how would she go through with tonight.

'You're late.'

Vanessa swept some hair behind her ear and, despite her stomach skipping rope, tried to look as casual as her outfit. 'Am I?'

When Mitch gestured her through into his home's foyer, she heard his smooth intake of air as she passed. 'My, you smell nice.'

'Thank you. Dog shampoo is so versatile.' She laughed at his raised brows. 'That was a joke.'

His mouth flattened. 'I'm a banker, Vanessa. We don't do jokes.'

Her heart stopped beating. 'Oh. I'm sorry. I thought—'

'Gotcha.'

His face broke into a gorgeous grin and she held off play-slapping his beautiful big arm.

He looked better than edible in jeans, a shade lighter than hers, and a worn T-shirt. The musculature of his chest through the soft grey fabric sent her heartbeat on a mile-a-minute sprint. As he turned away to usher her in, her gaze dropped to the languid motion of his easy stride. God help her, she wanted to slip her hands into those back pockets and *squeeze*.

She'd decided not to come tonight. She'd had every intention of calling this business meeting-cum-rendezvous off. They were from two different worlds, and she wasn't forgetting his mother on the war path. Her business difficulties must take priority... Coming here alone equated to courting trouble.

But curiosity had got the better of her and she'd crumpled. Excitement wasn't a big feature in her life. The idea of having a wealthy, handsome, eligible bachelor, who today had given off all the right vibes, was too intoxicating to resist. Didn't mean she had to go the whole nine yards and *sleep* with the guy.

As he'd said, they had work to do. Great and Small was her main concern. She wouldn't let anything— not even the temptation of dissolving into the magic of another mega-superb kiss—come before her number-one goal: saving her shop.

'I bet Kami's looking forward to seeing you again,' he said over his shoulder, waiting for her to catch up.

'You haven't heard the theory?'

'What theory?'

That fish had a five second memory span.

She waved a hand. 'Forget it.'

They crossed into the family room. The tank was on its own special polished wood unit. Kamikaze stilled before shooting back and forth and around his trident, an animated streak of shimmering gold.

Mitch laughed. 'Told you he'd be glad to see you.'

Vanessa smiled. Yep, one day he'd make a terrific dog owner—when he was ready to settle down.

'Did you bring your financials?'

Focused again, she held up a satchel. 'I brought

everything my bank manager asked for today—lease details, utility receipts, account numbers…'

She pulled up a stool at the kitchen counter, desperate to bite her nails while he flicked through the sheets.

'You're stuck in the red,' he noted after a quick perusal, 'and it appears you've already done what you can to cut costs and fend off creditors, which has artificially buoyed your cash flow.' His eyes met hers. 'Unfortunately, it's a tough time for small businesses.'

She swung her mouth to one side. 'Good thing I'm tough.'

Only she didn't feel so tough around him. She felt delectably weak and wonderfully female. There was something about a physically powerful, capable man that made a woman want to let go and melt right there against him. Not that she'd experienced this quality brand of euphoria before. Certainly not with her ex.

These heightened feelings were new. And nice.

Very nice.

He set the papers down. 'We should eat first.'

Her gaze jumped up from the pulse beating at the side of his tanned neck. *Get with the program, Vanessa.*

'Eat, then work.' She pulled up straight. 'Great idea.'

He brought four takeaway containers from the adjacent bench and laid out them out on a cutting board. Next, he retrieved plates, cutlery, linen napkins—his efficiency was impressive. How many 'clients' had he entertained here?

He flipped off the lids and she inhaled the mouth-watering bouquet of oriental spices and sauces. Chow mein, special fried rice, a Mongolian dish and sautéed vegetables. She would've chosen the same menu.

He reached for some goblets, visible behind a glass display door. 'Care for wine?'

'Alcohol and I don't mix.'

On her twenty-first, she'd been talked into knocking back a Tequila Slammer. She hadn't thought she'd be able to swallow it or, if she did, that it might come straight back up.

'Freshly squeezed juice, then.' He crossed to the giant stainless-steel fridge and found a glass pitcher.

After dragging up a stool beside her, he nodded at the feast. 'Dig in.'

'Do you have chopsticks?'

'Sorry. You're a fan?' He didn't sound surprised.

'One day, I'm going to take a vacation through Asia. Vietnam, Tibet. Enjoy the real deal.'

Then it was on to France, Italy and, finally, Greece!

He scooped some steaming rice onto her plate. 'You'll have a ball.'

'Do you travel a lot?' She dished out the vegetables.

'Some. I got a taste for it when I was young.'

'Family vacations abroad?'

Geez. Imagine that.

'When Dad could spare the time,' he stipulated. 'Before opening the door on the family business, he was an insurance executive, back in the days when premiums weren't through the roof and the small print was legible.'

As they ate, he topped up her juice and she considered the solid connection he obviously shared with the remaining members of his family. She could well imagine that Mrs Stuart leaned on him, and she was equally certain he would never turn his back and let any of them fall. He had *hero* written all over him.

She watched his jaw work as he set down his fork and reached for his glass.

'It's nice you're all still close,' she said.

His mouth twitched. 'Sometimes too close.'

Probably best to acknowledge Cynthia's plight. 'Your sister looked pretty washed out today.'

He frowned, then set down his glass. 'It's best. The guy's a chronic gambler. I can't see him lasting in the medical profession. I'm only happy he cut her loose.'

Nevertheless, Vanessa's heart ached for poor Cynthia. 'It's hard to be brave when you feel as if your world is folding in around you.'

Holding your chin high didn't mean you weren't still vulnerable inside.

He chewed, swallowed. 'Better to be hurt now than annihilated later.'

She forked around some bok choy. He was the family protector. The one the women relied on to know—and to do—what was best. Guess he had to be strong. Maybe a little too strong.

A horrible sensation whistled through her. She studied him as he finished his broccoli. 'Mitch, you didn't have anything to do with her fiancé's change of heart, did you?'

Had he paid the gambler off?

His scowl was deliberate but amused. '*No*. Although I'd like to send him a thank-you note.'

She sat back. 'You're one tough cookie.'

'Not too tough, I hope.'

Their eyes held, a glimmer of something more than understanding running hot between them. Overwhelmed by the intensity of his gaze—compelling yet at the same time almost cool—she dropped her eyes and forked around her fried rice.

Had he had a bad experience long ago? With an 'experienced' woman, perchance? Was that why his mother was so nosey now? Still, a man of thirty or so was free to make his own decisions, his own mistakes. How many long-term relationships had he had?

She set her fork down.

Talk about getting ahead of herself. She should escape while there was still time. She already knew what was on Mitch's more primitive mind, but far too many questions were whirling through hers to think straight; this minute only the quicksilver coursing through her veins whenever he looked at her seemed to make sense.

His BlackBerry beeped. He checked the screen and apologised. 'Do you mind if I get this?'

She blew her long fringe off her forehead. 'Not at all.'

Some distance would be good. It was getting a little hot in here.

While he took the call, she eased off her stool and rinsed her plate. He was engrossed in a conversation about signing papers, two week deadlines, everything being in order, no need to worry…

She drifted over to say hi to Kami and gave him a sprinkling of food. Then she spotted an open door. Looked as if Mr Stuart was the owner of a full-blown gym.

She glanced at Mitch, turned slightly away from her now, nodding as he concentrated on his call. No telling how much longer he'd be. He wouldn't mind if she had a quick look.

She wandered in.

The darkened room was spacious and featured a full-length glass wall, which presented a masterpiece of the harbour at night—colourful city lights hugging the dark velvet bays, the bridge twinkling magically in the distance. There was enough light from the hall to make out, directly in front of her, a rowing machine, a speed ball and a massive weight station.

A thrill rippled through her stomach. Muscles bulging, testosterone surging. She'd kill to see him hard at work on that.

A shadow passed over her, blocking out the light.

'Here you are.'

Her breath catching, she spun around. Mitch's silhouette all but filled the doorway—ominous, masterful. As a stir of apprehension weaved up her spine; she cleared the thickness from her throat and offered a shaky smile. 'I thought you might like some privacy, so I showed myself around. Hope you don't mind.'

He snapped on the switch and the room lit up. 'Make yourself at home.'

His eyes glistened with a not-so-secret smile. If she'd turned left instead of right, she might have come across his bedroom.

He joined her, picking up a dumb-bell from a nearby rack.

She smirked. 'You like to work out, or is all this to impress the girls?'

He didn't blink. 'Health is a priority. A little each day—'

'Keeps the doctor away.'

He laughed. 'Right. How about you?'

'I spend all day on my feet. I'm usually too bushed by the time I get home to think of anything other than a warm shower and curling up with a good book.'

Plus, however fashionable, she wasn't a fan of exercise. Never had been.

'You'd have more energy if you put aside even twenty minutes a day.' He handed over a weight.

Taking it, her overburdened arm flew down. 'You mean somewhere between sunrise and when I leave for the shop thirty minutes later?'

She rubbed her shoulder and he took the dumb-bell back. 'The kids are up early?'

She laughed. Her animals *were* her kids. She might only provide them with a temporary home but she loved and would remember every one who passed through.

He moved to the weight station bench. Looking up

the stack, he pulled to test a cable. 'Are the Rotties still there?' he asked offhandedly.

She didn't miss the deepened note in his voice.

'One of the females sold this morning.' But his buddy—the male—was still waiting for his perfect match.

Without further comment, Mitch collected two hand weights. 'Here. Try these.'

Against her better judgement, she accepted and curled her right arm at the elbow, then her left. Doable. But preferably not.

He knocked both fists against his pecs, *me Tarzan* style. 'Feel the oxygen breathing life through your blood?'

She surreptitiously scanned the length of his braced legs, his stellar athletic frame. 'I sure can. What's this for?' she asked guilelessly, indicating the mechanism at the end of the workout bench.

His eyes lit. 'Ah, this one's great for building the quadriceps.'

Quadriceps. She liked the sound of that.

To demonstrate, he reclined back on the bench, got comfortable, looped his legs around the two pairs of black padded cylinders and straightened his bent knees. As the denim around his thighs stretched, the cords in his neck strained, and Vanessa fought the urge to fan herself.

After a few more levitations, he unwound his legs and sprang up. 'You try it.'

She gaped. 'Who, me?'

Not only was she tragically uncoordinated, she was terrified she wouldn't be able to lift an inch.

As if reading her mind, he moved to the weight column and repositioned a pin. 'I've adjusted the weight. Now you have no excuse.'

She batted her lashes. 'Did I mention that in my final year I broke the coach's nose with a mutant hockey stick swing? After my javelin try out, the teachers unanimously voted to ban me from sport.'

He playfully crowded her back. 'Not listening.'

Beaten, she huffed and reclined while he hovered over her, checking those cables again. Her attention gravitated to the sinew and rock working beneath that T-shirt. His every movement proclaimed absolute power, Olympian authority. His mere presence took her breath away.

'Hook your legs between the cylinders,' he said, and she let him manipulate her lower limbs. Happy with her positioning, he stepped back. 'Now use your thighs and lift.'

Hands bracing her weight on the bench either side, she surrendered to her fate and lifted once, twice, three times!

Close to spent, she flopped back. 'And you do this for how long each morning?'

He rubbed the corner of his eye. 'Right after dinner isn't the best time for a workout,' he admitted.

She struggled to get up. 'I'll remember that.'

His hand grasped hers, warm and big. Maybe it was the rush of adrenaline from the impromptu exercise, but he overdid the tug. She flew to her feet, her nose landing inches from the beating hollow of his clean-shaven, exquisite-smelling throat. As her heart crashed against her ribs, her fingers begged to reach up and trail a sensual line around his shadowed jaw, then compare the rough to the soft kissable line of his lips.

Keeping her eyes straight ahead, she felt the burn of his gaze as his voice rumbled in his chest. 'You okay?'

She swallowed against a rush of raw physical need. 'A little out of breath is all.'

'Exercise'll do that.'

She dared to look up. His smile was sinful.

His arm came out to draw her near; she found the wherewithal to dodge and head towards the window. *Business and pleasure—gods and mere mortals—do not mix.* She was certain Mrs Stuart would agree. Mitch was tempting with a capital *Take me now*. But she was here to save her shop. Rescue the one tangible that had ever truly meant something in her life.

And then there was Mitch…

She stopped inches from the glass and its amazing twinkling view, wondering whether Kami, living out his existence in that tank, might feel a little like she did now. Restless…reckless…wanting something, yet not certain of the consequences should she suck in a big breath and go for it.

She could open her arms now and call to him. She was certain he would come. She could already feel the incomparable, never-to-be-forgotten hours ahead.

But if anyone ended up getting hurt in the end, hands down it'd be her.

Behind her, his natural heat radiated out, fanning new life on the kindling smouldering low in her stomach. His words stirred the hair at her ear. 'Guess we should go do some work.'

She couldn't quieten the pulse pounding in her throat. 'Work.' *Yes*. She nodded. 'Good idea.'

'I'd like to go through your P and Ls for the last twelve months.'

'And then?' She edged around and made the mistake of looking into his eyes. They were bright. Hot.

No doubt reading the yearning and indecision in hers, he tested, his hand skimming—barely a whisper—down her side. 'I'd like to look at your rent,' he said. 'Your location.'

The tips of her breasts grew to burning beads as his palm slid around to measure the rise of her hip. She fought to keep the pleasure from spreading lower and her eyes from drifting shut. 'Location's important.'

'If something you want is there right in front of you, it's hard to resist.'

His hot fingertips pressed into the small of her back, and her pelvis arced against him, melting wax against timeless stone. As if in slow motion, his head bowed over hers and his lips oh so lightly brushed hers, back and forth, up and down.

His warm wet tongue flicked the side of her mouth. 'Remember what I said about hard to resist?'

She succumbed to a sigh and admitted, 'Right this minute I can't remember my own name.'

She felt his wicked grin on her cheek. 'This is up to you.' His hands found hers as he walked her back till her shoulders touched the cool windowpane. He slid her arms out in a seductive arc against the glass so they came to rest either side of her head.

'If you're not sure,' he murmured against her temple, his body burning so close to hers, 'I won't push.'

The kindling in her belly leapt and sparked. 'Not even a little?'

His growing smile slid an erotic promise up around her jaw, leaving a wake of sizzling pleasure. His teeth found her earlobe, tugged, and the fire below burned more.

'Vanessa, I want you in my bed.' As her knees buckled, he caught her waist and held her hips against his—hard, insistent, irresistible. His voice lowered. 'What's the verdict?'

She took a deep, brave breath and dived in.

How could she deny it? 'I feel good about this.'

His blue eyes darkened. 'So do I.'

CHAPTER FOUR

As MITCH's eyes held hers, his burning fingers splayed down, winding around the hem of her T-shirt. Entranced, Vanessa lifted her arms and let the fabric glide up over her tummy, her bra, her head. No sooner had her shirt hit the floor than she returned the favour and his T-shirt joined hers by their feet.

In the stark artificial light, they both stilled, acknowledging the moment of no return. With his chest expanding fully on each breath, his head angled, then his gaze lowered to her lips. He leaned forward and their mouths lightly touched, touched again, and with each caress her need to have more went deeper.

Got stronger.

When he flicked her bra's clasp and slid the straps from her shoulders, the fabric of time warped and her surroundings dissolved. As each kiss grew less controlled and more fun, she surrendered to instinct, letting her palms fan over the delicious rock of a chest before searching out and fumbling with his jeans's button while he unzipped her fly. Hearing his soft groans, feeling his smile, aware that his hunger matched hers…

When had she thought she could stop this force from driving them together?

After they'd each kicked off their denim, his fingers twined with hers and he pinned her against the enormous back window. He first tasted a seductive path down her neck, progressed to her cleavage and around the aching peak of her right breast, then, with deliberate lack of speed, her left. His hands released hers to sculpt over her shoulders, over her ticklish ribs. She smiled as his palms moved lower, followed by his searching mouth.

Flexing her fingers through his hair, she revelled in the slide of his teeth as she burned white-hot inside. Delectable flames licked beneath her skin… oxygen evaporated before hitting her lungs…the connective cells in her body melted and all she wanted was to give herself to him, then happily die.

Crouching now, his knees either side of her shins, he peeled her panties down her thighs, his warm, skilful mouth trailing a thumping heartbeat behind. When she stepped out of the last of her clothing, he ground up against her, familiarising her with a sensory slide of his strength and furnace heat until they stood nose to nose.

The glass at her back no longer felt cool but rather *safe*—a transparent anchor to hold her against the torrent of giddy sensations casting her high. He cupped her cheek and kissed her again while his chest hair teased the points of her breasts and the room temperature jackknifed again.

She was light-headed—floating—when his lips eventually left hers. His heavy-lidded eyes gazed into hers, reaching so deeply she heard their souls whisper.

'I've thought a lot about this,' he murmured.

She sighed out a smile. 'That's nice to know.'

'I'd imagined going slow—' he grazed his lips back and forth over hers '—imagined making it last.'

She swallowed the groan of need pushing up her throat. *Make it last?* How much longer could she stand this sweet torture?

As if hearing her prayer, he scooped and hooked his pelvis under hers. Having peeled off his briefs when he'd ditched his jeans, his unrestrained erection gave a friendly nudge and the movement persuaded her thighs to part. She heard a hiss—his sharp intake of air—as his every muscle bunched and steamed.

Then he laughed, a low laboured sound. 'Know what I said about going slow…?'

As he spoke, he massaged her behind, manoeuvring her expertly until his tip pressed inside. The gasp of delight caught in her throat.

With a double grip, she clutched his jaw. 'Fast, slow. I'm not going anywhere—unless it's to your bedroom.'

He growled. 'Now we've started, don't think I want to wait that long.'

When he moved again and his engorged length filled her more, her mind went blank but for one simple glimpse at the truth. She only needed this feeling, this wild crazy spiral. Before now—before Mitch—she hadn't lived.

Without warning, he bounced her up and her legs automatically scissored around his hips. Now given the access they both craved, he took her mouth again and drove harder, plunged deeper, until the friction lit a candle so blindingly bright, a flurry of colour-filled sparks shot through her blood.

As her orgasm hit, intensified, multiplied—squeezing a mind-blowing beat—she clung to his neck and, over and over, murmured his name. In those few wonder-filled moments in time, nothing else existed.

Nothing else mattered.

All too soon the heady rhythm fell away. As the stars in her head faded, the visceral tension eased and she became aware of the fierce energy holding her close. His body trembled as the tendons between his shoulder blades locked, hard and slick.

Groggy, she drew slightly away. His eyes were shut tight. Did her warrior have a cramp?

'Mitch, what's wrong?'

He ground out, 'Forgot…condom.'

The light in the room suddenly got brighter. Protection was one thing no one wanted to neglect.

His eyes opened a crack. 'There's one problem. I don't want to let you go.'

That went double for her.

She had an idea to minimise the separation. 'How far's the bedroom?' If he had condoms, she guessed they'd be there.

He didn't answer but rather, understanding, turned up a wicked smile and proceeded to carry her through to his room, her legs still wrapped around his hips, his head buried in the grateful curve of her neck.

In the darkened bedroom, he carefully eased her back onto the cool quilt. She watched, awe-struck, as he retrieved a wrap from the nearby drawer, his superbly built frame working in the moonlight streaking in through the window as he prepared. She felt half sorry when the delectable show ended, but any disappointment vanished when he joined her again, seamlessly picking up where they'd left off.

Sinful yet also in some way sweet—his long full strokes rekindled those internal embers still aglow. She'd thought she'd been satisfied and he'd been on the brink, yet now he took the time to skilfully coax and love her, until soon she was leaping off that same mountain, freefalling into unsurpassed bliss with him close behind.

The drop was higher, the sensations clearer, and as the tingling ripples lessened and her spirit floated back, she knew no experience would ever top this, not if she lived a hundred years.

Afterwards he suggested a shower, where the water was warm, his kisses warmer and she learned that near nothing was forbidden between lovers.

Was it because he was a master of the game or because she'd been so attracted from the first? His strong arms felt as if they'd been created purely for her need and comfort. The way he adoringly soaped her back, the curve of her bottom, then up and down her thighs felt strangely familiar and yet all so new.

In the spacious black marble bathroom, they painstakingly dried each other with huge fluffy towels, then returned to the bedroom and burrowed beneath the fresh lavender-smelling sheets, gloriously naked and content. Yet already she wondered about next time.

About tomorrow.

At a twinge of guilt—they were from different worlds…she'd vowed not to succumb—she drew slightly away from the hard but comforting curve of his arm. Despite the hypnotic yellow glow of a corner lamp, she needed to push sexual compatibility aside and force her focus back upon the real reason she'd come to Mitch Stuart's home. She had a business, her home, to save.

'We should probably get up and go through those figures.'

His growl rumbled through her palm resting on the crisp hairs of his chest. 'I have a better idea.'

'What?'

'Let me hold you while you sleep.' His mouth twitched. 'Then again…' He rolled so that she lay beneath him, the tip of his nose touching hers. 'Who can sleep?'

When he'd finished kissing her thoroughly, his head kicked back as if he were coming to terms with a not unpleasant thought. 'I just had this amazing vision of you on my rowing machine.'

A laugh slipped out. She liked his adventurous

spirit but that was *so* not happening. 'You weren't listening to my school anecdotes, were you?'

She and sport were as compatible as oil and water.

His tongue drew a loving line around the shell of her ear. 'You're naked.'

She tingled and hummed as her fingertips weaved over his big shoulder, down the indentation of his muscled back. 'Of course I'm naked, silly.'

'I meant in my vision.'

He nibbled her chin. She closed her eyes and slipped back into nirvana. 'Mitch, I don't exercise, remember?'

His hot hand slid over her hip and between them. 'I think you do.'

Despite the drugging effects of his touch, weaving its spellbinding magic, she managed to tease. 'I far prefer intellectual pastimes.'

'I prefer you.'

When he kissed her, she kissed him back, again… and again…and again.

By 4:00 a.m., they'd made love twice more and Vanessa lay wide-awake on her side, watching her lover's darkly handsome face as he slept.

She would happily study him for ever—the faint scar below his left eye, the smooth bronzed rocks of his shoulders, the aura of animal magnetism that defined him even in his sleep.

Stopping herself from kissing his bristled cheek one last time, she eased back the sheets and slipped quietly out of bed. Through the smoky pre-dawn light, she stood, naked, willing herself to end the evening of her life and steal away.

Fresh wonder washed through her as, still asleep, a corner of his mouth curved and his arm moved from his side, his hand splaying out over the sheet as if searching for her warmth in his dreams.

She hugged herself. Lord, she wanted to snuggle back in. But she had to duck home and change before heading off to the shop. Chances were he'd want to see her tonight. But common sense and past experience said, as wonderful as it had been, this affair wouldn't last.

Water met its own level…no matter how great the temptation was to slip in and sleep with Mitch again, ending this now and protecting her heart was far wiser than facing the prospect of enduring poor Cynthia's acute strain of pain.

Mitch Stuart would be all too easy to love.

And lose.

She slipped into the gym, found her clothes and dressed, then made a detour to the kitchen. She collected her bag and, seeing the leftovers on the counter, remembered their first meal together; it seemed like someone else's lifetime ago. In the lightening shadows, she noticed a brown paper bag.

Fortune cookies.

Slipping her hand in, she selected just one. Then she tiptoed through to the living room, and Kami came to life. She bent and pressed her fingertip to the glass. 'Be good.'

Sliding the cookie in her jeans' back pocket, she stepped out and quietly clicked the door shut.

When would Mitch wake and realise she'd gone?

CHAPTER FIVE

LATER that morning, Mitch sat at the large, orderly oak desk, which had once been his father's, whistling as he organised his files for next week's board meeting, his last as Vice-President.

Not that his mind was on promotion today. His brain was stuck on a delicious groove that brought him back time after time to Vanessa's laugh, Vanessa's curves, Vanessa's moans and cries of pleasure as their lovemaking pitched them both farther out of orbit.

Either it had been way too long, or she indeed possessed powers that drew him in like the tide on full moon. His blood had ignited whenever she'd moved beneath him, or placed her lips on his skin—dear Lord, especially *there*.

When he'd woken, far later than usual, he'd been surprised and disappointed not to find her in his bed. He'd wanted to phone but instead he'd skipped his regular workout to spend time on the info in her business folder and put together a best fit financial rescue strategy. Within an hour of docking at the office, he'd had her loan in the pipeline. Tomorrow the money would be in her bank account. But tonight…

He twirled his pen and whistled again.

Tonight's agenda was pleasure only.

The office door flew open, threatening to fly off its hinges when the heavy wood slammed against the wall. As his father's solemn portrait rattled on its hook, Mitch lowered his pen and Garret Jeffson, acting President of Stuart Investments and Loans, stormed in.

The older man flung a set of papers on Mitch's desk. 'What the hell's wrong with you today?'

He'd spent a sensational evening with a woman in a million and this morning the sun had never shone brighter.

Mitch sat back. 'Nothing's wrong, Garret. I feel great.'

'Great or delirious? How do you explain this?'

Mitch recognised the papers, his signature. Vanessa Craig's loan application. He wouldn't ask how Garret had zeroed in on it so quickly. 'Honest Garret Jeffson' was straight as a die and possessed uncanny business instinct, reason enough for Mitch's father to entrust Garret the job, in the event of his death, of grooming his son for the top position. But Mitch had proven his competence, loyalty and commitment to Stuart Investments and Loans time and again; he did not appreciate having his authority questioned now.

Elbows on armrests, Mitch steepled his fingers under his chin. 'I've processed big loans before.'

Too many to count and way bigger than this.

'The applicant has no money, no assets, no guarantor. She's in debt up to her eyeballs. What the hell's supposed to be securing the loan—' Garret stopped, sharpened his gaze on Mitch's, then swiped his hand down his mortified face. 'My God, you're *sleeping* with this woman.'

Mitch's hands and expression tightened. He knew this job backwards. He'd lived and breathed this place for as long as he could remember. Day in, day out, and every minute in between. He didn't take kindly to being questioned now.

'That's really none of your business.'

Garret's fierce expression softened to fatherly understanding. He hooked a leg over the side of Mitch's desk and thatched his fingers on a thigh. 'Son, buy her a diamond necklace. Take her on a weekend trip to Paris. Don't put your reputation on the line—' his nostrils flared '—or this company's.'

'Garret, take it easy.' Mitch tried a wry grin. 'Just think, in less than two weeks you'll retire and won't need to worry about me or any of this ever again.'

Jowls turning as crimson as the carpet, Garret slowly pushed to his feet. 'Your father entrusted me to make the call on whether to promote you to top chair. I won't betray his memory or our investors' trust by going against my conscience if it tells me it's not time.'

Mitch studied his mentor's steely gaze. He'd learned so much from Garret. He trusted and genuinely admired this man above any other living. But

Garret hadn't interfered with his work in too long to remember. Mitch didn't like having what amounted to veiled blackmail held over his head now—and for no good reason.

However, he was also smart enough to know he had no alternative but to live to fight another day. After his thirtieth birthday, he would answer to no one. He couldn't wait to be free.

He grabbed his pen, swept the necessary instructions over the application's front page, then tossed the pen aside. 'There. I'm guarantor. No risk.'

Despite his earlier knee-jerk assumption about her financial dilemma, he believed Vanessa Craig had what it took. What was more, he intended to stand by and make certain that her troubled venture pulled through. Now he'd given her this loan, he'd steer her in the right direction. Relocation, of course, was a must.

With a knowing, almost smug look, Garret headed for the door. 'So it's true.'

'What's true?'

'Love truly is blind.'

Mitch felt the smack like a belt to the jaw.

He wasn't in *love*. He'd known Vanessa two days! He felt deeply about her, in a way that couldn't be explained to those who hadn't experienced the same roller coaster of emotions with someone of the opposite sex. What Vanessa and he enjoyed wasn't love—it was sublime pleasure.

He leaned back in his chair. 'I know what I'm doing.'

Hand on the door handle, Garret nodded as if he'd got what he wanted. 'Invite me to the wedding.'

When the door closed, Mitch cleared his throat.

Garret had it wrong. Marriage wasn't for him; he had enough family responsibility. What he wanted was a little fun. Hell, he'd almost forgotten what it was like to simply let go. And Vanessa was sexy and witty; better yet, she was independent, or had the potential to be. Which was a far cry from *dangerous*, which seemed to be Garret's implication. His mother's too, though that was no surprise.

When he was with Vanessa, his world felt…*enhanced*. So much so, he was counting the minutes until he held her again.

His gaze fell upon an invitation to a charity cocktail party this Saturday night. He'd already RSVPed, but he'd have his secretary call again and accept for two. In the meantime…

Picking up the phone, he pressed in a number and waited for the tinkle of her voice.

'Great and Small. How can I help you?'

A wave of endorphins burst through his blood. 'I can think of several ways.'

Mitch caught sight of his father's portrait looking down his long nose with a judgemental glare. He spun the chair away towards the city harbour view.

'Mitch?'

She sounded hesitant but also lawlessly sexy. He imagined her standing in her shop in her jeans and her T-shirt and his blood began to heat. 'How's the cockapoo adoption plans going?'

'They've had their shots and the breeder is sending some photos via email today. They sound gorgeous.'

He remembered the magic of her kiss. 'You're gorgeous.'

She made a modest noise that pumped his want for her that much higher.

'I take from that you're not annoyed I left without saying goodbye.'

'I forgive you,' he growled. 'Don't let it happen again.'

He expected her to laugh and was surprised when she didn't.

'Are you tired?' she asked instead.

He pitched his heels up on the desk and crossed his ankles. 'Never felt better. What about you?'

'I think I'll sleep tonight.'

'As long as it's with me.'

Her voice changed. 'Is that an invitation or an ultimatum?'

He grinned. 'Whatever works. How about we eat out tonight?'

He waited out two unexpected beats of silence. 'Actually, I'm expecting someone late this afternoon. I'm not sure what time I'll be free.'

Disappointment dropped through him like a giant lead weight. He blinked several times and came up with a solution—one that would have him seeing her as soon as possible.

'I'll drop in after closing time and see how you're doing.' A light on his phone lit—Garret's extension. His first instinct was to ignore it. Which was ludicrous.

Less than two weeks.

He threw his legs down and sat forward. 'Vanessa, I have to go. I'll see you around six.' Wondering who her visiting 'someone' might be, he frowned, running a palm over the approved application on his desk. 'I won't be late.'

'Aunt McKenzie!' Vanessa flung her arms out and pulled her aunt near. 'How wonderful to see you, but I was surprised when you rang this morning and wanted to visit. You hate the city.'

McKenzie gave her another quick hug, then stepped back and glared towards the broad front windows of her niece's pet store. 'Smog and traffic and too many folk. I haven't been off my property since—well, can't quite remember when.'

Vanessa walked with McKenzie through to the back of the premises, which she'd decked out with photos, favourite plants and a comfortable couch. It was near closing time; if someone entered the shop—including Mitch—she'd hear the bell.

All day she'd mulled over her decision to put the brakes on their intimate relationship. Again and again she'd reminded herself she wasn't in Mitch Stuart's league. Although she'd rather deny it, when push came to shove, chances were the downtown girl with next to no family and definitely no money would be little more than an entertaining interlude.

That didn't mean her heartbeat didn't skip whenever she thought of seeing him again.

Forcing her mind away from sexy Mr Stuart, Vanessa stopped with McKenzie in the centre of the back room. 'So, what's happened? Why the sudden visit?'

McKenzie set down her vinyl handbag and slid off her pristine white gloves. 'A dear friend called last month. We haven't seen each other since—' She all but sighed, then smiled softly. 'Since before you came to live with me. He's ill. I'm going to visit.'

Vanessa felt her expression open with surprise. 'Mac, that's so thoughtful. He'll be so glad to see you.'

McKenzie playfully snapped both her gloves over her left palm. 'So he should be. Flying all the way to Los Angeles.'

Vanessa's jaw unhinged. 'As in *California* Los Angeles?'

A smile danced in her eyes. 'My plane leaves later tonight.'

'I thought you were afraid of flying.'

That was what McKenzie had always said, and Vanessa knew why. Her parents had been killed in a light plane crash. Vanessa, not much more than a baby at the time, had miraculously survived, buckled securely in her child seat. McKenzie had kept her niece wrapped in cotton wool ever since.

Vanessa had loved her for it, but she'd also longed to spread her wings and experience life. To date, the ordinary girl from an ordinary town hadn't made it past Pitt Street. She wasn't discontented. As long as she could keep her shop, she shouldn't, and wouldn't, complain.

McKenzie dug into her bag. 'This is a super-quick stop. My cab's waiting but, before I go…' She withdrew an envelope. 'I want you to have this.'

Wondering, Vanessa took the envelope. Her birthday wasn't for months.

At first the large envelope appeared to be empty. She ferreted around and extracted, 'A cheque?' She ran an eye over the signature, then the amount and a hot chill dropped over her face and through her body. She swallowed. 'For a *million dollars*.' Had Aunt McKenzie robbed a bank? Done away with someone for insurance? 'Please tell me you're not running from the law.'

McKenzie laughed, a throaty chuckle Vanessa had missed very much. 'Remember your great-grandfather's painting he brought back from Europe?'

'You said it was an original.'

Obviously proud, McKenzie offhandedly toyed with one decades-old opal eardrop. 'I had an art dealer offer me a cool mill for it. I've sold the property too for round the same money, so half goes to you, half to me.'

Stunned, Vanessa pushed the cheque towards her aunt. 'You don't have to give me this. I can't accept.'

Aunt McKenzie's work-worn hands folded over hers. 'Nessy, I have no one in the world but you. I've never been flash. I prefer to be careful. And I've taught you to be careful too. So—' She thrust back her thin shoulders. 'Like Jim said, you can't take it with you when you go.'

'Jim's your friend?'

'The best.' McKenzie's pale green eyes glistened. 'We were engaged once.'

Vanessa dropped into the chair behind her. 'I had no idea.'

Her aunt was the classic spinster. She'd never spoken of former loves, had never seemed interested in men and now Vanessa knew why. She'd lost her heart to this man.

Mac's eyes searched Vanessa's, then she nodded as if it were time. 'After the accident and you came to live with me, I didn't have any room in my head or my heart for anyone's needs but yours. Jim was patient. For a long while he was. But I kept him waiting too long.'

Vanessa's hands went to her warm cheeks. McKenzie had given up her chance at real romance for love of her niece? No one could make a bigger sacrifice.

With a lump in her throat, she eased up and wound her arms around her aunt, the only mother she'd ever known. McKenzie smelled like the inexpensive powder she'd bought her every Mother's Day. McKenzie had insisted it was her favourite and didn't want anything else.

Vanessa bit her lip. 'Oh, Auntie, I'm sorry.'

Holding her niece, McKenzie patted her back like

she had when Vanessa's best ever friend had left in sixth grade. Vanessa had thought her life was over and McKenzie hadn't told her to grow up; she'd simply held her while she'd cried.

'You have nothing to be sorry for, sweetie. You've always been good. You've always made me proud.' She hugged her tight and murmured, 'There were times, so many times, I forgot that you weren't really mine.'

'Hello. Anyone in?'

Pulling back, Vanessa wiped her hot wet cheeks and focused through her tears on the doorway. She hadn't heard the front doorbell ring, yet Mitch was here, one foot pegged back, clearly worried he'd intruded.

She was letting her fantasies run away with her, but he looked so impossibly perfect, he gave her the most incredible butterflies, and when they were together…

Vanessa squared her shoulders.

She was a realist. But she was also an optimist. Was she being too hard on the possibility of *them*? Was it time she put past mistakes and insecurities aside and became optimistic about love? Aunt McKenzie's visit seemed to be a sign she shouldn't ignore. If someone hesitated and didn't grab for their chance, the man of their dreams could simply pass them by.

Moving forward, she took his hand and immediately felt reconnected—a key for her matching lock. 'Mitchell Stuart, this is my Aunt McKenzie.'

He tipped his head. 'Good to meet you.' He sent Vanessa a puzzled smile. 'I was under the impression you didn't have family nearby.'

'She doesn't.' McKenzie collected her bag from the table. 'My property was inland a ways.'

'Aunt McKenzie's on her way to the States.'

'In fact, I must get my saddle on.' McKenzie snatched a kiss and another hug. 'Have fun, kids.'

Vanessa laughed. 'You too.' It was high time.

'I'll see myself out,' her aunt said, slipping through the doorway that connected to the front of the shop. 'I'll visit when I get back.'

Vanessa remembered the envelope she held but Mitch's arms were already gathering her close. Misgivings about being left with that cheque and any lingering doubts about their relationship were replaced with sumptuous, explicit memories of the night before.

As his mouth dropped over hers, his warm palm cupped the back of her head, adjusting the angle enough to work a kiss that left her legs slightly shaky. When he reluctantly drew away, she was so dreamy, she barely heard his husky words.

'I missed you, Ms Craig.'

Her palm drifted up, fanning over the heat searing through the white shirt visible beneath his custom-made jacket. 'I like the sound of that.'

'I thought about you all day.'

She melted. 'Tell me more.'

The corners of his eyes crinkled. 'To save water and time, we're going back to my place first.'

'To shower before dinner, you mean?' She tingled head to toe and feigned a thoughtful look. 'That could work.'

'I'll tell you what else will work.' His hands slid

into her back jeans pockets. 'It involves post-dinner strawberries and warm chocolate dip.'

'Let me guess. In bed?'

He pretended offence at the same time that he shunted her hips closer to his. 'I don't like to be predictable.'

Surrendering to the sublimely inevitable, she snaked her fingers up through his strong dark hair. 'I'm willing to be surprised.'

Willing to be proven wrong.

His mouth had almost met hers again when Aunt McKenzie's frantic voice broke in.

'Lord above, Ness, there's someone outside who needs your help.'

The marrow in Vanessa's bones froze before she jolted into action. Mitch was already charging out.

'What's the problem?' he asked McKenzie, striding ahead through the store.

McKenzie didn't have time to reply. Mitch was already out of the door and coming to an abrupt halt as he stared down at a large tatty wicker basket. He swung a glance around at the inner suburban street and its busy pedestrians, moving patchwork shadows in the lights of passing cars.

'Anyone could've left them here.'

Her heart going out, Vanessa knelt on the hard concrete beside the basket. The mother cat, a tabby with frightened round eyes, growled to warn anyone thinking of harming or taking her five precious kittens. Half enthralled, half broken-hearted, Vanessa touched her fingers to her mouth. 'You poor darlings.'

McKenzie's tone was grim. 'Those kittens don't look more than a couple of weeks.'

Mitch squatted down. 'I'll take them in.'

As Mitch and his basket moved inside, McKenzie finished wiggling on her gloves. 'Seems like a nice fella.'

Handsome, strong, amazing in the bedroom. Vanessa nodded. 'Nice fits too.'

McKenzie stroked her niece's cheek. 'You deserve nice.' Then she sucked in a quick breath. 'And I need to catch that flight.'

Vanessa waved her aunt off in the cab, then scooted in after Mitch, locking the door behind her.

Mitch stood in the centre of the room, between curious Mr Cheese and the latest guinea pig family. He held the basket a little away, a look of mild discomfort stamped on his brow.

'Where do I drop them?'

She sent him a half serious scowl. He wasn't a cat person, but now was not the time for jokes. 'You can *place* them out back.'

He followed her through and settled the basket in a quiet, warm corner of the room next to her DVD player and stack of romantic comedies. They watched as the mother busily tended to each, making sure her clan was safe and well and clean.

Mitch absently looped an arm around her waist. 'Will you have the vet check them tomorrow?'

She instinctively leant her head against his shoulder. 'They all look healthy enough. I'll keep an eye on them overnight.'

'Meaning we're not going out to dinner?' She looked at him with an apologetic face and one corner of his mouth kicked up. 'I'll order takeout. How's Italian?'

She beamed. 'I *love* Italian.'

A loud mew shot her attention back to the basket. Releasing his hold around her waist, Mitch took a step closer. 'That little grey tabby…he looks thinner than the rest. Think he's hungry?'

'Maybe we should give him a bottle.'

He looked at her. 'Cats have bottles?'

She smiled. He had so much to learn. 'I have some kitten formula. But I might leave it a while and see. He does look smaller than the rest, but if she hasn't rejected him yet, there's not much chance of it now.'

The kitten continued to mew, then nudge at the mother's tummy, padding and searching out a nipple.

Mitch's frown eased. 'Damn. Never thought I'd be concerned over a basket of strays.'

The warmth in her chest transformed into a heartfelt smile. 'You don't like to be predictable, remember.'

He dropped a kiss on her brow, then gazed again at the basket and rubbed the back of his neck. 'So, are we going to sit up in a chair all night keeping watch?'

Floored, she stared at him. 'You want to stay and help babysit?'

He turned her in the circle of his arms. 'Lady, neither sleet nor hail nor howling cats could keep me away from you tonight.'

Longing spread exhilarating warmth through her body as she slid her palms over his shoulders.

'In that case, I'm willing to share my sleeping bag. It's a double.'

He smiled and drew her closer. 'That sounds ideal.'

CHAPTER SIX

Two hours later she and Mitch lay atop her pale pink sleeping bag, anticipating the rest of their evening alone—just them, the cats, Mr Cheese, the guinea pigs and a few hundred fish.

Mitch had gone home, showered, changed, and returned with penne and linguini dishes, as well as Italian salad with extra olives. After showering in the shop bathroom, she'd slipped into a change of clothes too—track pants and an *I Love Sydney* singlet.

They'd devoured the food and with full bellies now lay on their sides, snuggling spoon style, his front to her back, sipping soda water and quietly watching the mother cat and her babies sleep. Or she was. Mitch was more interested in finding new and fabulous ways for his mouth to caress her neck.

High on a cloud, her cheek on a palm, Vanessa reached back and wound his arm more securely over her waist.

'Wonder how long they'd have been out there if Aunt McKenzie hadn't noticed?'

Mitch lifted his head and chuckled. 'She's quite a character, your aunt.'

Vanessa smiled. 'She's difficult to describe. Strong on the outside, soft and sweet in the centre.' Like a cream-filled brandy snap.

Vanessa thought of the cheque and telling Mitch she didn't need to go ahead with applying for a loan with his firm. But all she'd known of life with McKenzie had been, of necessity, frugal. To be presented with a cheque for a million dollars out of the blue was mind-boggling.

Her aunt wasn't a liar. Still, Vanessa had the hardest time believing such a figure could be true. Before she said a word to anyone, she needed to be sure.

Besides, she didn't want to talk shop now. This moment—with Mitch's warmth so near and the atmosphere just right—was far too special to spoil with talk of money. Last time she'd confided in him about her financial state, he'd ripped up her card. She didn't want to think about that now.

'Aunt McKenzie gave me a home when I didn't have one,' she said instead.

His tone deepened. 'Did your parents kick you out?'

'They died when I was six months old.'

She felt his body tense. 'Ness, I'm sorry.' No one but McKenzie called her Ness. She liked the sound of it coming from his lips. 'I can't imagine never having known my parents.'

She pressed her lips together. 'I compensate.'

'By finding homes for others?' He grazed a tender

kiss over her temple. 'I'm betting one day you'll do even greater things.'

A beautiful sensation seeped through her chest. She'd never envisaged herself as a 'doer of great things'.

She looked over her shoulder at him. 'Really? How?'

He narrowed his eyes, half playful, half serious. 'Not sure, but I bet you'll find the perfect way.'

Did he mean it? For a moment, she was lost for words. 'Such blind faith.'

His eyes grew distant before his lips twitched. 'Maybe you've cast a spell.'

'Like the siren over her sailor?'

His smile held although his brow pinched almost imperceptibly. 'Should I watch out for rocks?'

A tiny mew came from the basket. They both pushed up on an arm, but all five kittens were curled around each other in a fluffy multicoloured ball.

Vanessa relaxed. 'One of them must've had a dream.'

He slid his lips along the receptive arc of her shoulder. 'Now the kids are all asleep, must be adult time.'

When she looked over her shoulder again, his mouth captured hers. The caress was slow and meaningful, making the blood in her veins thicken and heat. She would never tire of his mouth on hers. Never tire of having him near.

Lord, she really ought to rein in her emotions.

Shouldn't she?

When the kiss dissolved, she couldn't smother a blissful sigh. 'That's your thing, isn't it?'

He rubbed her nose with his. 'Kissing you is *definitely* my thing.'

'I'm talking about you racing to the rescue.' The protector. Her warrior.

'You mean the kittens?' He laughed. 'You make it sound so noble.'

'It *is*.' If she didn't know better, she'd guess he was a firefighter, or a doctor. Instead he was a highly successful banker.

Rolling completely over onto her other side, she faced him. 'You must love your work.'

He shunted her hips closer to his; his body language said he wasn't inclined to talk right now. 'I take over as President in less than two weeks,' he said, nipping her earlobe.

'That's *great*. Congratulations.'

'It's not final yet. One man can still veto the promotion.'

He stilled as if he were checking himself. Was she guessing right: that he didn't speak so openly with other women he'd only begun to date? That the super-highway conduit she felt buzzing and feeding between them wasn't imagination?

'This man,' she asked, 'he's some kind of enemy?'

'A friend of my father's, actually. Garret Jeffson.'

'Then what's the problem?'

'There hasn't been one…'

She carried the sentence through. 'Until recently?'

Pushing up on an elbow, he cradled his head in his palm. 'My father entrusted me to take care of the business and family. He went so far as to include as a condition of his will my performance at the firm. Only if I pass Garret's ultimate test do I win the chair.'

She remembered. 'Tough love. And you've rattled this friend's cage lately?'

'Yeah, for daring to have a personal life.' Thinking more deeply, he combed his palm over her hair. 'I live and breathe my work. Tonight I want to forget about responsibility.' His smile changed. 'Tonight I only want you.'

The backs of her eyes prickled. But, rather than gush, she tried to make light. 'The dog lady.'

When a brief shadow flickered over his eyes, she wondered.

Was he thinking about that Rottie pup? Wondering if he might have room in his life after all? She wouldn't tell him that a man had come in late today interested in the male for his son's tenth birthday.

But then Mitch's eyes sparkled. 'I have a function on Saturday night—a charity event. Come with me.'

She bit the inside of her cheek. 'Are we talking black tie?'

'Exclusively.'

'This might come as a surprise, but my wardrobe's a little light on Chanel.'

'Then we should shop.'

She theatrically clutched her heart. 'A man who *shops*?'

He grazed his sandpaper chin along the sweep of her neck. 'First time for everything.' He nipped a sensitive spot. 'Speaking of which…'

He slid his hand beneath her track pants' elastic and began to explore her in a way he'd never done before. As his warm fingers delved lower, she reflexively arched in, clutching and kneading his hard shoulder. 'Honestly, you don't have to do that.'

He looked up from nuzzling. 'I hope you're talking about shopping.'

When he resumed his attentions, his tongue trailing up her arched throat, her eyes drifted closed and she rolled onto her back. 'Shopping…yes… mmm…right.'

'Buying you a gown would make me happy.'

'You're easy to please.'

'I have a suspicion that I'm not. You just make it seem that way.'

He'd said it playfully, but when she opened her eyes she saw a glimmer of self-awareness in his.

As if a dimmer switch had been turned on high, her every sense seemed suddenly heightened. The sensation of his touch, the clock ticking on the wall, the clean musky scent of his skin.

His hand stopped moving. 'Is something wrong?'

She blinked and came to. 'I was just having a moment.'

His brows fell together. 'A moment?'

'You know. A special moment you want to lock in time and remember for ever.'

His chin went up in understanding. 'Oh, one of *those* moments. In that case—' he brought the top of the sleeping bag over their heads '—let's both remember this.'

The kittens woke her at dawn.

Dead tired, Vanessa rubbed her eyes, then saw Mitch gazing down at her, his weight resting on an elbow, his head in his palm, a lazy grin on his face.

He flicked a glance at the basket and deadpanned. 'I hate these early morning feeds.'

Remembering the glorious hours before, she stretched long and hard then, looping her arms around the broad column of his neck, brought his mouth down to hers. If the sound of mother cat licking and the baby cats clawing at the wicker hadn't been so intrusive, heaven knew how the embrace might have ended.

She let his lips leave hers and then shrugged. 'Looks like the world's awake.' Even if she'd rather not be. What time had they eventually got to sleep?

He pretended to frown. 'Do I have to go to school today?'

She wanted to laugh but covered a yawn instead. 'Unfortunately I really think it's best.'

Particularly given what he'd said last night about that 'friend' at his work and the coming promotion. She understood Mitch's reluctance; she too would love nothing more than to spend a decadent day in bed with him, but she had things to do. Most importantly, depositing that cheque.

He pushed back the cover and rocked up onto his feet. He seemed to have read her mind. 'So what's on your agenda today?'

As he sauntered to the kettle, checked the water and flicked the switch, she couldn't keep her eyes from the way the sinew in his back and butt and legs worked together, like a well-oiled, well-loved machine. Whatever he did on those regular morning workouts, she approved.

When he looked around and found his jeans, she knocked her dreamy self into gear and slipped on her trackies and singlet.

'I have a rather eventful day planned,' she replied with a secret smile.

'Well, find time to check your bank balance after 9:00 a.m.'

Yawning again, she rubbed an eye. What was he talking about? Did he know something about McKenzie's cheque? And that was only if she could believe it. But *she* hadn't even deposited it yet. 'What's up with my bank balance?'

His pecs bunched tight as he zipped his fly. 'I approved your loan application yesterday. The money would've been wired overnight.'

The shock struck, numbing her all the way through. 'I don't think I heard right.'

'We can clear your debts and start afresh with a healthy overdraft to play with.'

Her mouth didn't want to work. 'But I haven't signed any paperwork.'

'All fixed.'

'Is that legal?'

He hesitated, slotting his arms through his button-down's sleeves. 'I thought you'd be happy.'

'I *am* happy. I'm just…stunned. I wasn't expecting anything so soon.'

'We'll go over everything tonight and have you sitting high and dry by Monday.'

'I…' *Oh, Lord. Oh, no.* 'I don't know what to say.'

Chuckling, he slipped on a loafer. 'You say *thank you.* I say *you're welcome.*'

She held her spinning head. She had to sit down. 'Sorry. I'm still half asleep.'

Before she had time to blink, he was there, steadying her.

'I kept you up late again.' Bringing her close, he gave her a soothing hug, kissed her crown for a long moment, then moved away. 'I'll leave and you can catch another hour or so.' He jabbed a thumb at the basket. 'Tell that brood to behave till I get back.' He hesitated before leaving, coming back to steal another kiss that got stronger before he grudgingly let her go. 'I'll ring.'

When he left, Vanessa dragged herself over to make an extra-strong coffee. He'd gone to all that trouble, had processed the forms in extra-quick time. Who could've guessed that a miracle would take place: she had a cheque for a million dollars in her bag.

But it was so hard to believe. Her aunt wore the same Sunday best dress year in and year out. And the cheque wasn't a bank cheque but a *personal* cheque—it could very well bounce.

Mitch was a banker. If she showed him, he'd be sceptical too. He'd probably look at her as if she were, at the very least, gullible. At worst, nuts. So maybe she shouldn't tell Mitch right away that she no longer needed his loan. First, she would wait to be certain that the cheque truly represented what it stated.

A million dollars.

A mewing drifted out from the basket and she crossed to investigate. The runt, the grey tabby with a white-tipped tail, was clinging to the side of the wicker, trying to escape.

Setting her cup down, she gently collected the kitten in two hands, then held the ball of fluff to her chest. She stroked its wee head and it instantly settled. Another kitten was crawling up too. She squatted, her heart warming at the sight of the healthy little family.

'Any one of you guys want to tell me what I should do?'

All the kittens had shared a cuddle before she finally arrived at an answer. She hoped it was the right one.

CHAPTER SEVEN

LIFE just kept getting better.

After jumping in the car and visiting a couple of real estate mates with regard to better choice locations to re-establish Great and Small, Mitch strolled into his office some time past eleven.

He'd had a win as far as sourcing out sites that would offer improved expenditure without sacrificing on prime location. The couple he'd narrowed down to were in an upper-class neighbourhood, with affluent passing trade. The space was on the small side; Vanessa would have to cut her stock by at least half, and there was no back room. But the trendy, slick operation he had planned—dealing more in boutique and corporate pets—needed a minimum of floor space.

Tonight he would explain the pros and cons; he was sure she'd be excited. But, for now, he had some administrative catching up to do.

Inside his office door, Mitch whistled as he shrugged out of his jacket. Turning to drop it over the coat stand, his buoyant mood dipped when he noticed Garret Jeffson sitting behind his desk.

In his chair.

Checking his cufflinks, Mitch assembled his thoughts and moved forward. 'Morning, Garret.'

The older man rapped his fingers on the solid timber desk. 'Where have you been?'

Disagreeable heat surged in his gut but Mitch found a temperate smile. 'Clearly I've been out.'

'You missed the meeting with Vanmir Strivers.'

'I briefed Vanmir yesterday on my opinion regarding our groundwork interest in expansion into Australasia. I let him know I'd be out this morning. I also left a message with your secretary in case you were looking for me.'

'Then you turned off your phone.' Garret exhaled and shook his head. 'This was an important meeting. I'm not interested in excuses.'

Mitch's right eye twitched and he crossed his arms. 'Why do you think I'd feel a need to make excuses?'

'You're avoiding my question.'

Mitch kept his voice low and calm. 'Where I've been is none of your business.'

'You're wrong.'

Mitch dropped his arms. 'And you're sitting in my chair.'

Garret's stern expression eased. 'Your record is exemplary. I'm willing to overlook these last couple of days, but, Lord above, Mitch, I was young once too. I know the signs. You've picked the worst time to go fall in love.'

Amused, Mitch hacked out a laugh. He was *not* in love. And, 'I'm not a teenager. I'm an accomplished businessman who's earned a track record of running this corporation beyond successfully.'

'Be that as it may, you're not home and hosed yet. I must have a clear conscience when I hand over the chair.'

Setting his knuckles on the timber, Mitch leant over the desk.

'What's that, Garret? A threat? You're going to hold that miserable clause in my father's will over my head now?'

He was conscientious like Garret, honourable like Garret, but, *hell*, he deserved a life! He made decisions for everyone else. Surely he could make his own.

Garrett patted down the air. 'Son, I understand the pressure—'

Not wanting to listen, Mitch shut his eyes and concentrated on summoning his usual cool self. When he had it together, he straightened, exhaled and walked around his desk. 'I have work to do.'

Garret evaluated him before pushing to his feet. 'My wife took ill last night. She's in hospital. The doctors believe she's had a series of mini strokes. I need to cancel my meeting in the Melbourne branch this week. I'd like you to go in my stead.'

Mitch blinked several times, absorbing each section of news. Feeling like a prize heel, his shoulders slumped. *Damn.*

'Garret, I'm sorry.' He rubbed his forehead. 'Go be with your wife. I'll look after Melbourne.'

Garret's mouth moved, perhaps to say thanks. Instead, he put a hand on Mitch's shoulder. 'Don't ever forget, I believe in you, son. I know you'll do what you have to and come through.'

He shut the door behind him.

For ten minutes, Mitch strode up and down the length of his office. Garret meant well. And of course he'd go to Melbourne; Garret needed to be near his wife. But Garret had to understand Mitch Stuart was no longer a kid, hadn't been for too long. If for the first time in his life he wasn't acting himself, so *what*.

He'd been an adult since he was fifteen, tied down to 'head of the house and family and business'. Now, damn it, he deserved a little freedom.

The portrait on the wall caught his eye. His hands bunched and flexed before he strode over and unhinged his father's portrait from the wall.

'Sorry, Dad. Time to do things my way.'

'Wow.'

That Saturday night, standing before an obviously appreciative Mitch Stuart, Vanessa proudly swirled the skirt of her one and only, real life evening gown. Not having seen Mitch since Tuesday, she'd spent the afternoon at a beauty salon and felt as though she ought to be on the cover of *Harper's Bazaar.*

She hitched up a shoulder, cheeky but also coy. 'So, do I get a pass?'

'I like you in jeans but…' He rubbed the back of his neck. *'Wow.'*

Her laughter bubbled up.

Even standing here, at the doorway of her lacklustre granny flat, she felt like a princess. She'd never owned a dress anything like this divine creation. Shoestring straps looped from the outer edges of a soft bodice that resembled an open clam shell. The airy skirt, which drifted down from high on the waist, fell close to her body…until she moved. Then the aqua jewelled silk floated out, as the shop assistant had noted, like glistening waves on the sea.

It had cost way too much, and she didn't regret a penny of it.

Her smile faltered, however, when Mitch glanced past her shoulder. Her flat was small, lacking personality, really quite drab. But she'd always viewed it as temporary, a place to lay her head. She spent most of her time where she most felt comfortable—her shop. The place she preferred to call home.

'No need to come in,' she said quickly. 'I'll get my things and we'll go.' She swung back to grab her bag from the hall stand.

'Don't rush. My driver can wait.'

Driver? 'Does that mean I get to ride in a limo?'

She turned back. With more distance between them, the full effect of his extraordinary presence took her breath away. His tuxedo was classic, cut to fit his superior masculine frame to a perfect T. Black tie suited him. Well, of course it would. He was born to wear Armani with an air of entitlement, yet he did it with such effortless style.

She studied his hair. Was it combed differently, or had it merely grown? Dark licks touched his collar the barest amount. She couldn't wait to run her fingers through and muss it up a little.

She grinned.

Actually, a *lot*.

This unexpected five-day, four-night separation had been agony. She'd been so disappointed when he'd rung to say he needed to fly to Melbourne straight away. Looking back, how austere life had been before him.

With a sultry grin, Mitch reached for her arm. Crossing the threshold, she happily joined him and went to descend the two unpainted steps. But he held her back, winding his arms around her waist and tugging her close for a pulse-racing kiss hello.

Her senses buzzed and swirled and ultimately became one with his.

Oh, yes, she remembered this feeling…

With his eyes still closed, he released her, groaned and then pretended to shake himself awake from his trance. His satisfied smile roamed her face. 'What were we saying?'

Feeling lighter than air, she took his arm. 'Your driver.'

'Ah, yes. We do, indeed, have a stretch limo tonight,' he replied, heading down the steps. 'My friend appreciates if his guests put on a bit of a show.'

'It's a charity event, yes?' He nodded. 'What does your friend raise money for?'

'The annual cocktail party raises funds to support fledging entrepreneurs.' He arched at brow at her. 'A timely event for you.'

As he escorted her down the cracked cement drive, Vanessa spotted overweight Mrs Micheljon and her hair rollers peeping through a bent kitchen blind. At her landlord's curiosity, a moment of doubt hit—Little Ness Craig from the country in fancy dress. Who was she fooling?

But then she remembered how special she felt in her evening gown, walking beside this incredible man. She lifted her chin and held onto his arm all the tighter.

'I make a sizable donation each year,' Mitch was saying as they headed towards a gleaming black stretch; a fully uniformed driver stood by the passenger back door. 'But all the organisation and distribution of funds is Thomas's baby.'

The driver's salt-and-pepper moustache twitched as he smiled at Vanessa and opened the door. Feeling like Cinderella—had the driver of the pumpkin coach been a horse or a dog?—she sat back and soaked up the otherworld luxury of polished wood grain, softest leather, even a mirror-shine champagne bucket, complete with two sparkling flutes.

Lowering himself beside her, Mitch reached for the bucket. She was waving her hand *no* when he pulled out the bottle—her favourite label lemonade.

She laughed as her heartbeat fluttered.

He'd thought of everything.

Before the limo pulled out from the kerb, he poured and raised his flute to hers. 'Here's to my beautiful companion.'

She *tinged* her flute with his. 'And to my handsome escort.'

Sipping the sweet bubbles, she remembered McKenzie's cheque had been cleared yesterday. Now was the right time to let Mitch in on her news. She didn't know if she'd ever felt more excited. More proud. More *nervous*. How would he take the fact that she was a millionairess?

Lowering her glass, she cleared her throat. 'Mitch, there's something I need to tell you.'

'Let me guess. You overspent on the gown. Don't worry.' His blue eyes flashed over the rim of his glass. 'I'm disappointed I didn't get to go on that shopping trip, but let me know how much I owe you for the dress. Whatever the cost, it's worth it.'

She dropped her gaze and slid a palm over the jewelled silk. She knew he was only keeping his word—he meant well—but something about his offer now made her almost uncomfortable. 'I'm glad you like it, but I don't want your money.'

He set down his glass. 'If it's about your shop,' he went on, 'I researched some properties earlier in the week.'

'Properties?'

Now she had her own funds, she intended to stay where she was. The biggest drain on her finances was rent. If she *bought* the premises, earnings could be funnelled directly back into the store. She'd even indulged in a wild dream about eventually buying the whole street. But, realistically, it would be more than enough to keep the place that she'd built a thousand happy memories around. Thanks to Aunt McKenzie, it actually seemed possible.

'The properties are a bit smaller,' he said.

Her question was automatic. 'How much smaller?'

'Not much less than half of what you have now. And no back room facilities,' he said quietly but firmly. 'That's hardly a necessity anyway.'

She was gobsmacked.

His knee hooked onto the seat as he angled more toward her. 'The two spaces I've narrowed it down to are in a great neighbourhood. Lots of people with lots of money to spend on the very best.'

She pushed against the hollow ache in her stomach. She liked where she was.

Although she didn't want to sound ungrateful for all his time and thoughts, her disappointment came out sounding like irony. 'Mitch, if I'm meant to be responsible for a loan, shouldn't I get some say?'

Concentrating on the limo slowing and pulling up, Mitch only half heard her question. Vanessa peered out of a tinted window. Were they there already?

The door swung open and a tall, attractive man, with a straight nose and liquid brown eyes leant into the car. 'Mitchell Stuart Esquire, how the dickens are you?'

Mitch moved across and they bear hugged on the pavement before he turned to help Vanessa out.

'Thomas, this is Vanessa Craig.'

'Your exquisite date for this evening.' Thomas made a performance of kissing her hand. 'Pleasure's entirely mine. Your gown is delicious.'

Mitch sent her a wink.

Thomas gestured at the wide tier of steps behind them that led to an opulent function room—Grecian columns, giant marble pots and strategic falls of colourful landscaping framing the building like a picture.

'Go through and mingle,' Thomas said. 'Champagne's going round. Canapés too. Dancing's to come. Hope you're staying for the fireworks.' Another limo pulled up and Thomas waved at the occupants. 'I do love these nights.'

As Thomas strode off, Mitch linked his arm through Vanessa's and escorted her up the steps.

'Yes,' he offered, 'Thomas is gay.'

She inclined her head. 'He's charming.'

'And a great business brain. If I weren't so tied up with the bank I'd like to work on something more with him.'

Once inside, a couple swept up to them—a business associate of Mitch's from a legal firm and his wife. A leading computer analyst, then a controversial politician came next. Soon several others had joined their circle.

What she caught of the conversation was stimulating, but when asked her opinion on the new trend in Parisian fashion, then the decline in world economic stability, she didn't know quite how to reply. Mitch kept her close and must have thought she was enjoying herself. But it seemed everyone knew each other so well and were speaking a language only those in the clique understood.

After a couple of hours, her smile began to ache. Stupid, but she was homesick, wondering about her kittens, particularly Roger, her little grey tabby.

When she shifted her weight and her shoes pinched her toes so much that she flinched, she tugged Mitch's sleeve. 'Would you excuse me for a minute?'

He frowned. 'Something wrong?'

'Not at all,' she fibbed. 'I want to go powder my nose.'

He dropped a lingering kiss on her cheek, close to her mouth, then returned to the conversation.

Feeling outside the bubble—*adrift*—Vanessa wandered out onto the balcony. She needed air. More than that, she needed to get out of these five-inch heels!

At times she felt so right with Mitch and yet here, in his world, she felt…alien. The feeling had been the same at his mother's house. Out of her depth. A tolerated intruder.

On the balcony, she gazed out over the glistening black harbour, which danced with colours reflecting off the surrounding city lights. Bending, she slipped off one shoe, then the other and groaned as she wiggled her freed toes.

She'd hoped—had very nearly *convinced* herself, in fact—but who was she kidding? Mitch enjoyed her company, and he'd gladly made a concession tonight.

But shouldn't he be with a woman who knew and loved this language—the nuances of *glitz and glamour*?

He'd confirmed as much that first night when he'd torn her business card in two. He hadn't wanted her kind—ordinary folk who lived from pay packet to pay packet—infringing on his world. But then, at his mother's house, he'd kissed her again and she'd found herself swept away…willing to believe…

When a warm hand settled on her shoulder, she jumped, spun around and held her racing heart.

'*Mitch*. It's you.'

His eyes glowed darkest blue as he smiled. 'So this is where you got to.'

Letting out a guilty breath, she didn't bother to hide the shoes in her hand. 'The view's just so beautiful.'

He kept his eyes on hers. 'Yes, it is.'

Her stomach muscles clenched. Oh, God, this must be—*he* must be a dream. The moment she dared think otherwise, she would wake and know handsome millionaires didn't inhabit her world. Not on a long-term intimate level, anyway.

He ran his warm palms down her arms. 'You're shaking.' He claimed her hand and turned towards the connecting French windows. 'We'll go inside.'

She bit her lip, but then said it anyway.

'Can we stay out here a little longer?'

He edged back around and searched her eyes. 'Then I'll warm you up.'

He wound his tuxedo-clad arms around her, tucked her in and began to sway to the music filtering out from the ballroom. Vanessa could have swooned. Their first dance.

His cheek resting against her temple, he breathed in and melded her closer to his heat. 'Mmm, that dog shampoo really works for me.'

A laugh slipped out. 'See. You're just too easy to please.' But her voice didn't carry true conviction when she said it this time.

He brushed his lips over her crown. 'You want to leave?'

She inwardly groaned. Darn it, no matter how out of sorts she might feel, she had to go back inside. She couldn't ruin his night.

'No, no,' she assured him. 'I'm fine.'

He tugged her away, looked into her eyes, then said more firmly, 'We'll go.'

She hesitated but finally conceded. She'd been told she should never play poker.

They said goodbye to Thomas and a few other guests then resumed their seats in the back of the limousine. As the vehicle pulled out, Mitch gave her his full attention. 'Now, we were interrupted earlier. What did you want to tell me?'

She sat up straight and ploughed right in. The sooner it was out, the better. 'You know my Aunt McKenzie?'

His expression twisted. 'Don't tell me she's found more cats.'

Her laugh was edgy. 'No. She sold her property as well as a painting that belonged to her grandfather. She got quite a sum for it.'

His teeth flashed as he smiled. 'That's great.'

'She wanted me to have it.'

'All the money?'

'Only from the painting.'

He nodded carefully. 'I see. How much are you talking about?'

'Four times the amount your firm loaned me.'

After a moment, his jaw shifted. 'When did you learn about this?'

'The night you met McKenzie.'

He looked as if he didn't quite believe her. 'And you said nothing?'

Her explanation tumbled out. 'I didn't quite believe it at first. It was a personal cheque. I wondered if it'd go through. Then you told me about the loan approval when I was still half asleep and left the state that day. The cheque only cleared yesterday and I wanted to tell you in person, so… well…' Out of breath, she shrugged. 'I'm telling you now.'

When he merely nodded again, she went on. 'I want to pay out the loan.' His nostrils flared. 'I know there'll be fees attached,' she acknowledged quickly. 'I'm happy to pay whatever's involved.'

His face hardened. 'You think that bothers me?'

His eyes shifted from hers as if he were thinking something through.

She frowned. 'So what *is* bothering you?'

'Nothing.' His lips pressed together.

'Mitch…what aren't you telling me?'

'Nothing serious. Nothing that makes a difference.'

She had a bad feeling. She wouldn't rest until she knew. 'Please…'

A pulse in his neck throbbed before he rolled back one shoulder and admitted, 'I went guarantor for you.'

The statement sank in like a stone plummeting to the bottom of a well. The loan had been processed in the blink of an eye, without even a signature, when three other institutions had turned her down flat. But never in her wildest dreams had she thought he would as good as put up the money for her. At that time they'd known each other only two days.

It was lovely.

It also made her feel naive. Duped. Possibly even bought.

Hadn't she told him at the outset that she didn't want to be treated like a charity case? She'd never wanted to feel patronised or paid for. Was she right to feel hurt? Embarrassed?

Her neck and face began to burn. 'I was a bad risk—I knew that—and yet you let me believe something different.'

He exhaled, almost wearily. 'I went guarantor because you believed in your future.'

Which he'd thought malleable enough to steer towards a tiny space in upmarket Snobsville. He didn't understand what that modest pet store meant to her and that she would do everything in her power to stay. But then why should he understand? They might have slept together but in reality they were little more than strangers. Two people with different values from totally different worlds.

Still stinging, she murmured, 'You should have told me.'

His expression was less than amused. 'And you should've told me.'

As a withering feeling leached from her middle, she looked away and sat back. So, here it was: the first crack…the first indication Cinderella was back from the ball.

She'd fumbled her way through tonight, but Mitch would fit better with someone who was clued up. Who laughed at highbrow jokes. Who knew the best wine. Who didn't live in a tumble-down house, but rather habitually flew to Hong Kong to shop. Someone he truly respected, not inadvertently patronised.

She was just another flighty female who had the potential to be a drain on his time. The million dollars she now had in the bank couldn't change that.

She fought the urge to hold her pounding head. She needed to get home before her gown turned to rags.

Long moments of silence dragged out before the limo parked outside the house attached to her granny flat.

Mitch swung open the door. 'I'll come in.'

She put her hand on his thigh and fought the urge to react to the steely warmth. She wouldn't meet his eyes or the tears edging hers just might fall.

'Please, Mitch. Don't.'

She was aware of his chest rising, falling, then his hand scrubbing his jaw.

Finally, he nodded. 'I'll call tomorrow.'

He let her pass and alight onto the pavement. She heard him rap on the window, which separated passengers from the driver, then listened to the door shut.

As the limo purred off, she clutched her bag to her bodice, willing away the sensation of her heart breaking in two.

Would he call tomorrow?

Should she have let him in?

If he didn't call, if he was so damn easy to put off, wasn't it better that this was over now?

Feeling as lifeless as the unwatered daisies in the garden, she slipped off her shoes, picked up her hem and trudged down the path. She ignored Mrs Micheljon spying through the window. She only wished she could ignore the crushing pain beneath her ribs, the tears building in her throat.

She'd reached the steps when, in the still night, she heard an approaching noise—the purr of a car.

Her grip tightened on her bag and she spun back in time to see the stretch limo reversing up. Before it stopped, the door fanned open and Mitch leapt onto the footpath. He strode down the drive until they stood a foot apart, then he swept her up into his arms. Without a word, he headed back to the road.

Overwhelmed, near speechless, she struggled to find her voice. 'What on earth are you doing?'

His tone was deep and determined. 'Consider yourself kidnapped. You're coming home with me.'

'But Mitch—'

He stopped and his hot kiss swallowed her words.

When her bones had liquefied and delicious hope pumped again through her veins, his mouth gradually released hers.

He held his unswerving gaze on hers. 'You were saying?'

She pressed her tingling lips together as a pitifully relieved tear slid down her cheek. 'I don't have a change of clothes.'

He continued to walk. 'You won't need one.'

Arriving home, Mitch sank into a plush living-room chair and impatiently wrenched his bow tie to release the knot. Vanessa stood before him in her shimmering gown, looking unsure, like a wide-eyed vision only the most privileged of men got to see.

He snapped open his collar stud.

Did she have *any* idea?

She'd been quiet on the drive here—as had he—both mulling over the relationship-altering events of the night. Each had been taken aback. In hindsight, they should have shared what they'd learned tonight earlier. When the wall had gone up, he'd knocked it down quick before a molehill of misunderstanding had the chance to grow into a mountain.

But Vanessa appeared so fragile standing before him now, he had to ask.

'Do you want to be here?'

In the soft down light, her eyes glistened, a reflection of her exquisite gown. 'If I didn't, I would've said so.'

'Maybe I wouldn't have listened.'

It was said in jest, yet the deepest primal part of him laughed and said it was true. Every day he'd spent in Melbourne had seemed like one more day lost. He'd managed to keep his mind on business nine to five, but when night had fallen he'd been sorely tempted to jump on the earliest jet and fly home.

And that was crazy.

She was a woman—a tempting, beautiful, enthralling woman. But nothing and no one had ever had a detrimental effect on his job performance. As he'd told Garret, he wasn't a teenager. He might be taken with her, but work had to remain his priority.

He'd got through the time away by looking forward to tonight. Some ruffled feathers over a loan wouldn't upset this time now.

He pushed to his feet. Before he uttered the words, he imagined the result of his unashamed request.

'Ness…take off your gown.'

Her lips parted and her eyes widened more before her lids grew tellingly heavy. The movement of her breasts—her breathing—quickened. Then she crossed her arms high and eased the silk strings off her shoulders. She reached behind and he heard the murmur of the gown's zip easing down. The silk slipped, exposing her firm, rose-tipped breasts, before the dress fell in a rush, a soft layered bundle at her feet.

With his heart banging in his chest, Mitch drank in the heavenly symmetry—her perfect breasts, the hand-span waist and, lower, a V of aqua silk that covered that most feminine sacred part of her.

He shrugged out of his jacket, tossed it on the chair, and went to her. He let her sweet scent fill him, savoured the heightened anticipation, then he took her hand and led her to his room.

Her hand in his, Vanessa was surprised when Mitch stopped before reaching his bed. In his room, they stood before decorative strips of floor-to-ceiling mirror. Naked, but for her panties, Vanessa allowed herself to be turned in his arms until she faced her reflection, her fully clothed lover, his black bow tie hanging, standing behind.

His unhurried gaze wound up her legs, her hips, lovingly caressed her breasts and finally, in the mirror, found her eyes. She held her breath and trembled as his expression intensified and his hot hands moulded around the column of her neck. His fingers tightened slightly, then fanned out, sculpting over her shoulders, her arms, making every inch of her flesh burn and catch light.

His touch roamed across her abdomen before his hands climbed to measure and weigh her heavy breasts. Her heartbeat pounded as he drew a teasing circle around each areola then gently rolled the hyper-sensitive peaks. She tried to maintain their eye contact in the mirror but, when he rolled harder, she surrendered to the overwhelming thrill and let her neck arch back.

She moaned in her throat as his lips moved against her hair. 'Say my name.'

Arching into his touch, she swallowed and tried to think straight.

'Mitch,' she breathed.

His right hand slid down to clutch the V of her panties and drag them to one side. With deliberate lack of speed, one finger spliced between her folds, curling deep inside her before slipping up again. Pressing her against him, he circled that pulsing spot while his other hand rolled and pinched and she went up in flames.

His hot breath warmed her cheek. 'Say it again.'

The words spilled out. 'Mitch…oh, God, Mitch… you're driving me mad.'

'Like you drove me mad last week.'

Through her building delirium, she grinned. 'So, this is your payback.'

'This is our reward.'

He whirled her around and, kissing her as if it were the first time, walked her back towards the bed. When she lay upon the sheets, he pulled her panties off, then undid his shirt, one agonising button at a time.

Not soon enough, he joined her.

She coiled her legs around his thick thighs, urging him to a powerful pace until every plane in his body gripped tight and shuddered with release. When his breathing steadied, he rolled on his side. Taking what

he knew of her body and her mind, he rocked her—
loved her—until she, too, shot deliciously high and
over the edge.

CHAPTER EIGHT

THE next morning, in a red silk suit, Mrs Stuart descended the stately steps of her home and greeted her son with a possessive hug.

'You look as handsome as ever,' she declared before shifting her attention to Vanessa, who already itched with prickles of discomfort.

Mrs Stuart extended her hand. But, before Vanessa had time to accept the token gesture, the older woman whipped her hand away to hold her cheeks in delight.

'Do I hear the baby barks of my cockapoos?' Mrs Stuart cried.

Vanessa closed her eyes and wished herself away.

After the cocktail party and her fantasy kidnapping last night, she'd woken in the tangled sheets of Mitch's bed. This morning, neither of them had needed to rush off.

Following another luxurious hour of 'Mitch magic', he'd tried to coax her into the gym to participate in his morning workout. When she'd protested, he'd instead shown her the indoor pool. There, amidst the echoing quiet and smell of salt and chlorine, he'd coached her in the art of water play—minus swimsuits, of course.

Later, at Great and Small, she'd introduced Mitch to the new junior she'd hired during the week, after she'd been sure her shop would survive. He'd pretended not to be too interested in the Rotties while she'd checked on the kittens—Roger mewed the loudest—and the cockapoo breeder had arrived.

All four pups were silky pale red in colour, but each was unique in temperament. Nicknamed Sleepy, Sneezy, Dopey and More Dopey—MD for short—the littlest was just a hopeless bundle of fun and energy.

Although everything seemed fine and wonderful on the outside, and Vanessa was relieved they'd got over their hiccup regarding the loan he'd organised and her confession about Aunt McKenzie's money, the connection between herself and Mitch seemed to have changed. The way he'd looked at her when she'd brushed her hair this morning. How he'd studied her hand, rubbing her thumb with his, moments after they'd made love.

The difference was almost imperceptible, except to say that the purest essence of what they'd shared had been altered.

She felt closer and yet…

Well, must be she was still coming to terms with this past week: accepting she might lose her shop, meeting Mitch, being gifted that money from McKenzie and, last night, discovering Mitch had withheld the fact he'd taken personal responsibility for the loan he'd organised.

Little wonder she'd felt overwhelmed and over-sensitive.

Now, delivering the cockapoos to Mrs Stuart didn't help. Vanessa was happy for the pups; they'd be loved and well cared for. But, man, she couldn't wait to leave. Being here, amidst this overt grandeur and Mrs Stuart's haughtiness only scratched at those feelings of inadequacy and not fitting in that, last night, Mitch had managed to caress and kiss away.

Striding back towards the vehicle, Mitch answered his mother. 'The pups are in the back.'

Mrs Stuart clasped her hands under her chin as Mitch opened the tailgate of Vanessa's CRV. 'Let's each carry one in, shall we?' She turned towards the house and called, 'Cynthia, the dog lady's here!'

Vanessa sniffed.

A coincidence? She thought not.

In a casual lemon dress, Cynthia appeared and hurried down the steps. Unlike the last time they'd met, she greeted Vanessa with a sincere smile. Her blonde hair looked and smelled freshly washed and there wasn't a handkerchief in sight.

'I'm looking forward to meeting the new family members.'

Vanessa returned Cynthia's good vibes. 'They're looking forward to meeting you too.'

They each collected an excited parcel from the carrier; the puppies were wiggling bundles of joy.

This was what Vanessa most loved about her job. Every time she found a great home for one of her pets, a tiny piece of her found a home too.

Not that she could see this place ever taking on that meaning for her, the knowledge of which only served to stir up those nagging insecurities again— the deeper understanding that Mitch's world and hers couldn't be more different.

Vanessa mounted the stairs with MD in her arms, wishing she weren't counting the minutes till her escape. As they traipsed through the house, Wendle and her mousey overbite were drawn from her polishing by Cynthia's laugh: Sneezy was scrambling up Cynthia's bodice, desperate to lick her nose.

Out back in their room, Mitch closed the door. The four lowered their puppies, then stood back while they sniffed and scampered around their beds and balls and bowls, a different colour for each.

Cynthia sighed. 'Thank you, Vanessa. They're just gorgeous. I feel a thousand times better already.'

As Cynthia moved away to play with Dopey and Sleepy, Mrs Stuart slipped up beside Vanessa and said, for her ears only, 'It's wonderful to see Cynthia smiling again. Sometimes it's difficult to let go, but when relationships are damaging…' She gave a resigned shrug.

While Vanessa bristled, for herself as well as Cynthia, insensitive Mrs Stuart flicked her a glance.

'We have some settling up to do. Would you follow me?'

Vanessa looked for Mitch. He was playing with

Dopey and a tug toy so, with her next belt of oxygen, she sucked down some courage too. She didn't need Mitch to face this woman. She'd provided a service. If Mrs Stuart didn't approve of her personally, frankly, too bad.

Except, if she and Mitch continued to see each other…

She shuddered.

The idea of a mother-in-law like Beatrice Stuart curdled her blood.

When she and Mrs Stuart reached the living room, the slant of Mrs Stuart's lips aptly conveyed her sense of superiority. 'I was right.'

Although her heart *ka-thumped* wildly, Vanessa kept her face a mask. 'About what?'

'You *are* experienced.' She moved to a credenza to collect what looked like a cheque. 'We're very happy with the puppies.'

Vanessa didn't allow her gaze to waver. 'Mrs Stuart, is there something you want to say to me?'

The older woman's smile spread. 'You're direct.' She nodded. 'Good.' Cheque in hand, she bent to smell the credenza's vase of scarlet roses. 'I had a visit yesterday from Garret Jeffson, my husband's closest friend and interim President of his bank. Mitch is scheduled to take over the lead reins at the end of the week. Unfortunately, after some uncharacteristic behaviour these past days, Garret's concerned Mitch isn't in a sound place mentally to assume such a responsible position.'

As Mrs Stuart collected a pair of mini secateurs from a hidden drawer to prune some thorns, Vanessa let the information sink in. When she continued to prune, Vanessa pushed.

'I take it you're blaming our relationship for Mitch's…mental state.'

Mrs Stuart turned her acid smile on her guest. 'When do you suggest we have the puppies spayed? I don't want strays chasing my precious babies. I'm sure the breeder would agree.'

Vanessa's throat clogged. Where did this woman get off? 'Mitch wouldn't appreciate this conversation,' she said with remarkable restraint.

'Perhaps not today. Just as Cynthia didn't appreciate her broken heart last week.' She waved the secateurs towards the back room. 'But you see she's feeling so much better. It was the right thing to do.'

As realisation dawned, slow and vivid, Vanessa's head tingled with the truth. Mrs Stuart had thought Cynthia's fiancé wasn't truly good enough, just as *she* wasn't good enough for Mitch.

Her face twisted in disgust.

'You paid Cynthia's fiancé off, didn't you?'

Mrs Stuart set down the pruners and joined her. 'I want you to look inside, Vanessa. I want you to put Mitch's well-being before your own…ambitions.' Vanessa opened her mouth, but Mrs Stuart hurried on. 'And, before you tell me you aren't ambitious— my dear, any woman worth her coiffure wants to better herself. I understand that. I'm merely concerned that you're trying to conquer Everest when you should, perhaps, be content tackling territory closer to home.'

Vanessa coughed out a humourless laugh. 'You're unbelievable.'

Any scrap of pity she'd felt over this woman's loss of her husband was, sadly, well and truly gone.

'You care about my son,' Mrs Stuart went on, a beseeching note to her voice now. 'I can see that. So do I. I would sacrifice myself to see him achieve his best. That's the truest measure of love.' Her mouth pursed. 'He needs to get his mind back on business or risk losing the reward he's worked towards and deserves after fifteen long years. My dear, you don't want him to resent you later for getting in the way. And, let's be honest, that resentment *could* surface as soon as next week.'

Vanessa closed her mouth. She hated that Mrs Stuart had touched a nerve—*two* nerves, in fact. Aunt McKenzie had shown the truest measure of her love when she'd sacrificed Jim to devote herself to her newly orphaned niece.

On top of that, secretly, Vanessa was waiting to wake up and have Mitch realise that her vastly different history and circumstances might make her an interesting interlude but cancelled her out of competing in any long-term stakes. One day—maybe as soon as next week?—she expected Mitch to have had his fill and say goodbye.

Like a hound scenting blood, Mrs Stuart went on.

'Please, take the time to consider it. To acknowledge that Mitch needs someone beside him who understands the establishment. Who can help with the social aspects, who went to the right schools and talks to the right people.'

Vanessa's thoughts wound back to how out of place she'd felt among the ridiculously rich and famous last night, then to how her affluent ex had considered her 'fluff on the side'.

Mrs Stuart was nodding as if she had a direct line to Vanessa's unspoken doubts. She handed over the cheque.

Feeling like that poor country orphan all over again, Vanessa looked down at the cheque. And tried to shake the disbelief from her head.

Her gaze snapped up. 'This is far too much.'

Mrs Stuart's soft hand settled over hers. 'Call it a bonus for a job well done. I don't believe we'll be needing you again.'

Mitch's deep voice broke into the nightmare.

'Formalities over, ladies?'

Mrs Stuart's face lit up. 'I think so, yes.'

Mitch moved to Vanessa and, smiling, threaded some hair behind her ear. 'Do you want to say goodbye to the pups?'

Vanessa's tongue felt swollen and useless in her mouth. She swallowed twice, then pushed out the words. 'No, no. I'm sure they'll be fine.'

'In that case—' Mitch moved to brush a kiss on

his mother's cheek '—we'll see you later. Go join Cynthia. I've never heard her laugh so much.'

'You won't stay for lunch?' his mother asked.

'Not today.'

Mrs Stuart didn't look concerned. 'Next week then.'

With Vanessa's new assistant minding the shop, on the way back from his mother's house, Mitch suggested they stop for lunch at Manly Beach.

Vanessa's appetite was non-existent, but they'd skipped breakfast so she knew Mitch must be starved. With burgers, chips and colas in hand, they found a bench and table on the fringe of the white sand. Vanessa donated most of her lunch to the gulls, who waddled and flapped in a noisy, ever-growing mob. But the food she did manage to get down, combined with the fresh, salty air and tranquil blue sky, helped to regenerate her spirits.

Aunt McKenzie's fondest saying was: believe in yourself and surround yourself with others who believe too.

After last night she'd been willing to give Mitch the benefit of the doubt—that his intentions towards her went deeper than merely *here and now*. Mrs Stuart's poisonous words had eroded a good measure of that belief. Sitting beside Mitch now, Vanessa was certain of only one thing.

No matter how long she and Mitch dated, she never wanted to see his mother again. It was a long way from cowardice or stubbornness. It was self-preservation. Some people—and their prejudices—she simply didn't need in her life.

And yet a voice inside her persisted in pointing out that at least *some* of Beatrice Stuart's argument made sense. Vanessa did care for Mitch. She did want what was best. But wasn't she—*this*—best for him now?

Or was she merely an untimely distraction who might jeopardise his future?

Vanessa pushed against her pounding temple. Oh, she was sick of thinking and rethinking. And if she spoke with Mitch about this second private conversation with his mother, she'd come off sounding like a whiner. Or maybe even being manipulative herself. Mitch didn't need the aggravation.

Mrs Stuart might consider her a would-be-if-she-could-be. She didn't need to dignify that insult by giving it another voice and sharing it with Mitch.

She was here with her handsome, vibrant lover on a glorious spring day. She was damn well going to enjoy it.

Throwing the last chip to a squawking gull, she inhaled deeply. 'Doesn't the ocean look wonderful?'

Mitch finished his can of cola. 'I was thinking the same.' He nudged her. 'Wanna go for a dip?'

She gave him a wry smile. 'We don't have swimsuits.'

'Didn't stop us this morning.'

'Except now we're in public.'

'You're right.' His hand slid up her leg, beneath

her dress. 'Let's go back to my house and I'll teach you how to bomb dive.'

She caught his hand, but then inched it higher. 'Sounds a little energetic—' her mouth twitched '—but fun.'

'The fun comes when we're both underwater.' He shunted closer and his cola-cool mouth lowered and found her breastbone. 'How long can you hold your breath?'

'How fast can you run?' Vanessa jumped up. 'Let's go down to the beach.'

She wanted to sprint as fast as she could, which didn't happen often. In fact, had never happened before. She had an overwhelming urge to run free!

Looking pleasantly surprised, he bent and slid off his loafers. She kicked off her sandals and bolted off ahead, down onto the warm, soft sand.

'Hey!' he called out. 'Wait for me.'

Turning around, she jogged backwards and sing-songed, 'You can't catch me.'

He picked up speed. 'The heck I can't.

She squealed as he hurtled towards her, kicking up sand as his legs pumped across the clean stretch of beach. When he was almost upon her, she dodged, swerving towards the giant curls of teal water.

She found enough breath to laugh. 'Sorry, but I thought you were fit.'

His big chest heaved as his eyes narrowed. 'Know what I think?'

'What do you think?'

'I think you want to get wet.'

He edged towards her, a menacing glint in his eye.

On a flash of panic, she held up her hands and tried to reason. 'Mitch, listen to me. We don't have a change of clothes.'

His grin was unconcerned and fatally sexy. 'You're always on about clothes.'

She looked down. Lacy scallops of cool water swirled around her ankles. 'It's cold in here.'

'It'll be invigorating.'

She raised her hands higher. 'I give up.'

'Too late.'

'I'll make it worth your while.'

He lunged towards her. 'I know you will.'

Laughing, they fell at the same time a wave crashed and tumbled over them. How he found her lips in the powerful foamy rush she couldn't guess. She only knew he was right. It *was* invigorating.

And she was in love.

When they arrived back at the shop, thanks to some towels in the back of the CRV, she and Mitch were more damp than wringing wet. And Vanessa was still alight with optimism. She wouldn't think about nasty mothers. She would concentrate instead on the coming days, hours and minutes she'd spend with the man she adored.

Would it be too hopelessly absurd to think—to hope—that he might fall in love too?

He was a grown man; he could and should make

his own decisions, as should she. And they'd decided to be together. They wanted to enjoy the ocean, and the laughter, and the—

'…last of the Rotties sold, Miss Craig.'

Halfway to the counter, Vanessa stopped dead. She studied her new assistant's bright expression as her greeting sank in.

'Lucy, you can call me Vanessa, remember.' She glanced back to see Mitch squelching in through the entrance of the shop, his chinos dark in patches and his black hair drying in wisps. He stopped by the glass pen holding the last Rottie.

Vanessa turned back to Lucy and lowered her voice. 'But the male's still there.'

Lucy and her nose ring leant forward and innocently mimicked her boss's conspiratorial tone. 'A man came in and left a deposit. Said he'd be back week after next to pick the puppy up on his son's birthday.'

Having caught up, Mitch set his hands on Vanessa's shoulders. Behind her, none the wiser, he asked, 'What's up?'

Vanessa was about to say *nothing* when Lucy announced, 'I was just saying the last Rottweiler's gone. Or will be. The man who left the holding fee had such kind eyes. The puppy wanted to leave with him there and then. He said he'd spoken with you before, Miss Craig.'

Her back still to Mitch, Vanessa closed her eyes as her stomach dipped and looped.

'Oh. Yes. I remember now.'

Mitch's hands left her shoulders. 'Well, guess the little guy found the right home.'

Dreading to see his expression, she edged around. They'd known each other a week; did she have any right to believe he'd changed so much so soon? That he'd been contemplating—even looking forward to—bother and fuss and noise.

That he was ready for more.

She squeezed his hand. 'I'm sorry, Mitch.'

He dismissed it. 'I'm fine. I'm good.' But his easy smile didn't quite reach his eyes.

Efficient Lucy wasn't finished. 'And a lady called.' Her long purple nails collected a message from next to the cash register. 'A Beatrice Stuart. She said the cockapoos are doing fine.'

Vanessa wanted to block her ears, not to news of those pups but the sound of that name. 'Thanks, Lucy.'

'She also left a message for someone called Mitchell.' Lucy turned her hazel eyes on Mitch. 'That's you, right?'

Mitch held that unconvincing smile. 'I'll call her tomorrow.'

Lucy rattled the note. 'But this is *about* tomorrow. The lady said,' Lucy read carefully, '*Mr Jeffson has called a meeting regarding Australasia and the chair. He hasn't been able to get you today. You need to be in the office by 7:00 a.m. sharp*—'

Mitch interjected. 'Got it. Great. Thanks.' His face was tight when he gestured towards the back room and said to Vanessa, 'I'm dying for a coffee. How about you?'

Out back, Vanessa peeled off her dress while, pre-occupied, Mitch flicked on the kettle, then stared blankly out of the window at the alley's brick wall. She retrieved two towels and handed him one. Absently fluffing her hair, she moved to the single-door wardrobe to fish out a change of clothes.

She found the jeans she'd left there earlier in the week, as well as fresh underwear and a T-shirt. Moving to the small adjoining bathroom, she spoke to him through the open door.

'Your mother's message sounds serious.'

She imagined that he shrugged as he grunted. Then came the tinkle of a teaspoon as he prepared instant coffee.

She slipped on the new underwear and T-shirt, then, curious, ducked her head around the corner and saw him staring out of the window again, dripping teaspoon poised above one of two cups.

'You're going to that meeting, aren't you?'

Thrusting back his shoulders, he inhaled. 'I've been in touch with Garret more than a few times last week. He's just edgy...trying to make a point.'

'About you having a personal life?' she ventured, knowing Mrs Stuart would love the fact she felt responsible.

He grunted. 'As for my mother, leaving that message, here of all places—' He threw the spoon in the sink. 'I'm too old for Simon Says.' He sipped his coffee, frowned and poured the rest down the drain. 'God, I hate instant.'

Remembering the million-dollar coffee machine in his mother's mansion, Vanessa's stomach knotted as she blindly found her jeans and slipped one leg in. 'It's only another week. Maybe you should—'

She stopped when his eyes caught hers. They weren't smiling.

'Vanessa, I can handle this. I've known this man all my life.' She slipped in her other leg as he came to her and set his big hands on her hips. His tone softened. 'Don't worry. This has nothing to do with you.'

The blood rushed to her feet.

How wrong he was.

He caught a kiss that didn't linger beyond a few seconds. 'You finish getting changed. I need to get out of these trousers.' He set his forehead to hers and held her gaze. 'Come over later. I'll look after dinner.' He smiled. 'It's getting to be a tradition. What do you feel like?'

She smiled weakly. 'Maybe Thai?'

He wiggled her hips. 'Extra-hot.'

As he left, Mrs Stuart's words reverberated through Vanessa's mind…

He needs to get his mind back on business or risk losing the reward he's worked towards and deserves after fifteen long years. My dear, you don't want him to resent you later for getting in the way.

Turned inside out, Vanessa sank onto the chair

behind her. Her pocket crunched. Wearily, she reached behind and found the shards of that fortune cookie she'd forgotten about.

She pulled out the squashed cookie, along with its words of wisdom, and read:

When you see another with a contrary character, look inward and examine yourself.

Terrific. Why couldn't it have said, *Remember to brush your teeth after meals*?

She wandered over to the kittens and collected baby Roger.

As much as she didn't like Beatrice Stuart, they had one thing in common. They both wanted the best for Mitch. But, although she believed she and Mitch were entitled to this time, it was as flattering as it was obvious…

She *was* a distraction.

A potentially dangerous one.

For years, Garret Jeffson had wielded a cane over Mitch's head, its full length inscribed *tough love*. Last week, she'd apparently unleashed a streak of pent-up rebellion in Mitch that wouldn't be silenced, even when he knew there could be consequences.

But she had the power to stop this battle of wills from getting worse. If Mitch stuck to his guns and refused to play the game as his mother and Garret Jeffson directed, what was to stop Garret from withholding the Presidency of the bank from Mitch indefinitely? Maybe Mitch would end up telling them all to go jump. If she had indeed been the catalyst, how would she live with that?

Burrowing her cheek against Roger's little head, she looked inward and knew what to do.

CHAPTER NINE

'WELL, now, this is a surprise.'

Feeling the rapt smile stretch across his face, Mitch stood back as, an hour later, Vanessa crossed the threshold. Jeans, T-shirt, blonde hair loose and shining, face clean of anything other than its natural glow. He was taken back to that first night—was it only a week ago? A life-altering, unforgettable week he couldn't have anticipated when they'd first met. She'd been so different from any woman he'd ever dated. This evening she looked fresher and more tempting than ever.

He tugged his ear.

Even if that particular pair of jeans was ready for the rag bag. And looked *sensational* on her because of it.

If that new girl, Lucy, was in the shop tomorrow, perhaps they could get to sleep in.

Mitch flinched.

Except for that meeting. If Garret's wife hadn't been ill, he'd have no hesitation believing tomorrow had purely been devised to see if he'd jump. And the harder Garret turned the rope, the less inclined he was to play.

Some people might call that pig-headed. Mitch called it finally making a stand, even if, yes, the timing was inopportune.

'I bought some supplies.' Vanessa held up a green carrier bag.

He gave her a playful scowl. 'You don't have to bring groceries here. Anyway, we're having Thai.'

'Guess again. I'm going to cook.' His brows shot up as she brushed past. 'Hope you like soy burgers.'

Was she serious?

He shut the door. 'Actually, I prefer mine with ketchup.'

He chuckled but she spun around and tapped his nose. 'Wrong answer.'

Feeling a little off balance, he followed her into the kitchen and, succumbing to the hot pulsing tug in his gut, wrapped his arms around her slender waist, nuzzling her neck as she prepared to unpack the carrier bag. She'd been on fire down at the beach today. Sexy and reckless and teasing beyond reason. Good thing they *had* been in public or she'd have been in real trouble.

He ground against her.

Then there was tonight…

Waiting for the moment she'd melt against him and turn around, he stopped tickling her lobe with his tongue when he spotted a foreign object on his counter.

He broke away and took a step back.

'Lentils?'

She frowned over her shoulder at him. 'You like to keep healthy, right?'

He edged forward and tugged open the bag. 'What else have you got in here?'

She smacked his hand and wiggled her brows. 'Magic ingredients.'

As she busied herself unpacking again, understanding dawned. He spun her around and crushed her against him until she must have known how strongly she'd been missed.

'Ness,' he growled, 'you don't need to impress me. Deep down, I'm a man of simple tastes. Three veg and a big steak more than does it for me.'

She looked disappointed. 'No steak, I'm afraid. But I do have carob rice-cake tarts for dessert.'

Horror dropped through him. What was this? Cravings? She couldn't be pregnant. Either way, no matter how much he wanted to please her, cardboard smeared with fake chocolate was not up for discussion.

Anyway, who was hungry?

Getting back on track, consciously stoking the kindling that smouldered down below, he steered his hands down her sides while he tasted her temple, her cheek.

'We can cook tomorrow night if you want,' he murmured. 'I've already ordered. This restaurant has the best Pad Thai in town.' He lowered his head to sample her sweet mouth. 'Hot and spicy.'

When he felt her teeth tug her lip, he drew back

to see she looked more sulky than worried. 'Can I say I'm a little tired of takeout?'

His head snapped back and he blinked several times. All he could think to say was, 'I see.'

The doorbell rang at the same time that off-balance feeling pushed the back of his knees in again. He drove a hand through his hair and headed for the door. 'Guess the delivery guy's early too.'

They ate at the dining table, Kami blowing bubbles and looking on. Mitch only opened his mouth to eat, mainly because Vanessa wouldn't keep quiet.

Halfway through the meal, he had the absurd feeling she might be pulling a joke. Was he being filmed for *Punked*? But, hell, basically he was happy to listen to her voice, all night long if she wanted.

He got his wish.

Long after dinner, the chatter kept coming. Some time around eleven he decided she could continue her dialogue in a different part of the house.

He pushed to his feet and held out his hand. She took it, looking uncertain. 'What are you doing?'

'Going for a walk.'

As he pulled her up she caught the time on her watch and exclaimed, 'Oh, gosh, look at that. No wonder I'm bushed. We've both got big days to-morrow. Perhaps we should…'

He slanted his head over hers and kissed the words away. When she surrendered and relaxed, he swept her up in his arms and didn't let go his silencing lip-lock until he'd moved through the gym and reached the edge of his indoor pool.

Their mouths softly parted. Her eyes were drowsy with longing as she sighed, 'Where are we?' She frowned and sniffed. 'I smell chlorine.'

'Remember that bomb-dive lesson I promised?'

Her lidded eyes opened wide. 'Mitch…no. You *wouldn't.*'

Her last word came out a howl as he pitched her into the drink. He waited for the splash, then bomb dived in too.

Geronimo!

Mitch slept like a log and jumped out of his skin when Vanessa woke him at dawn, shaking his shoulder, then leaping out of bed to go brush her teeth.

Scrambling up on an elbow, he scrubbed his sleepy face.

After their skinny dip last night, they'd climbed into bed some time after one. Was she on steroids? And, if she was, how about coming back and sharing some more of that energy around? He day-dreamed about the limitless joys of their morning sex…the first rays edging in through the blinds, the curlew crying from afar while they pleasured each other front to front, head to toe and, his favourite of favourites, Ness on top.

But something in Vanessa's frantic brushing in the bathroom told him that wasn't on the cards today.

A moment later, she breezed out and proceeded to

choose a shirt and tie from his wardrobe. Frowning and scratching his chest, he pushed up higher.

Okay. This was weird.

His laugh was short and he wished he hadn't forced it. 'Ness, settle down. You're not my mother.'

Already dressed, she turned from the tallboy, a pair of socks in each hand. 'Oh, I know that.'

He patted the mattress three times. 'Stop flitting around and come back to bed.'

Still on her sock mission, she didn't seem to hear.

This was getting beyond weird.

His voice lowered. 'Ness, what's going on?'

When she turned to him, she looked almost offended.

But, come on. She was acting like… Like a *wife*. He didn't *want* a wife. Or a cook. Or even a chatterbox. He wanted a lover.

He wanted his Ness.

She dumped his socks atop the tallboy. 'I have to leave really soon,' she said. 'I have some new Rotties coming in today.'

Mitch ground his back teeth. She knew he had a thing for that Rottie pup. Why mention a new lot now?

'I wonder if you could come to the shop?' she went on. 'Say, around nine and help me bundle up a couple for an important customer who lives a little out of town. You were such a help yesterday with the cockapoos.'

Air turned to icicles in his lungs. All he could think was, *Was I so wrong about her?*

His words grated out. 'Yesterday was Sunday. Today's a work day.'

When he flung back the covers, her clasped hands flew to her chin. 'Mitch, God, I'm sorry. That was so dumb of me.'

Her eyes were so big and green and beautiful. Without grabbing his robe, he went to her, unable to help wishing that she was still naked too. Irritation forgotten, he curled a knuckle around her cheek. 'Don't worry.'

She smiled, pleased that he'd forgiven her. 'Maybe you could come over later in the afternoon, then. Four would be fine. Three would be better.'

His right eye twitched, he dropped his hand and headed for the bathroom. 'I have meetings today.'

From behind, he heard, 'Oops. Of course.'

Brushing his teeth, he caught the time on his watch. If she was heading off, he'd have time for a workout before getting to the office at seven.

He rinsed, then splashed his face.

God, he wished this week was over.

When he returned to the bedroom, a towel lashed around his hips, Vanessa stood by the bedroom doorway, her eyes uncertain. She looked cornered… or guilty.

Mitch's heart twisted.

Hell, maybe this was just a bad morning. Maybe he needed to wake up. Maybe he should get this week done with—get his priorities straight—before switching his attention to other things.

He went over, cupped her face and his mouth met hers. She coughed a little and drew back. 'Sorry.'

Smiling, he went to kiss her again, but she barked out another one. He stepped back and frowned. 'You ought to watch that cough.'

She held her throat. 'I do feel a little scratchy. Tea's supposed to be good for colds. I'll get one at the shop.'

In a blink, she was gone, leaving him standing there with that weird off-balance feeling happening again, as if he were standing on the slippery deck and the ship was listing.

About to go under.

Mitch got to the office five minutes before seven. Garret was waiting. The meeting went smoothly—no surprises, no hiccups. The Australasian expansion plans were discussed and the chair handover was set to go ahead Friday. But, for the entire two hours, Mitch was sidetracked, thinking about Vanessa.

That afternoon around three, Mitch picked up and fast-dialled Great and Small.

Lucy answered. 'Vanessa's out the back with a lemon tea. I'll tell her you're on the phone.'

A full five minutes later, Vanessa croaked down the line, 'Hey, Mitch.'

He shuddered. 'You sound awful.'

'I'm coming down with something bad. Do you mind if we don't see each other tonight?'

He drew a circle on his day pad and cocked a brow. 'I could bring over some lozenges. Massage oil with eucalypt is said to work wonders on the respiratory system too.'

She coughed so loudly, he pulled the receiver away from his ear. 'I feel like rolling into bed and sleeping for a week. In fact, I was about to pack up now, go home and die.'

He slashed a cross through the circle. 'Do you want me to drive you home?'

'You're busy.' Those words sounded livelier, firmer, but then she coughed again. 'I'm fine to drive.'

'I'll call tomorrow, then.'

But the following day it was the same story, only she didn't make it to her shop. Over the phone, she sounded as if she were talking past needles stuck in her throat. He pushed back his office chair. 'I'm coming over.'

She wheezed, then sneezed. 'I look terrible. *Feel* terrible. I just need to hide away in my cave until I'm well.'

He hated to give in. He had to do *something*. A big bunch of spring flowers seemed a good plan.

The next day she told him, 'I'm getting better but I don't want to infect you.'

He drew three straight lines on his day pad. She didn't sound any better.

He sent a bigger bunch, roses this time. When Thursday came and went, the doubt monsters began to bite. She could have TB or some deadly strain of bird flu. Then another voice whispered, *And she could be avoiding you.* He hadn't forgotten her odd behaviour last Sunday night and the following morning. Was this all connected?

By Friday, Vanessa wasn't answering her phone and Mitch was unstoppable. He wanted answers. Was she truly sick? Or was his gut feeling right: she was putting on the voice and the symptoms in order to avoid him? If she no longer wanted to see him, he would deal with that. But he wasn't living in this limbo any longer. Not knowing was doing his head in.

Garret stopped him in the hall on his way out. 'Mitch, do you have a moment?'

Mitch silently cursed before manufacturing a smile. 'Not right now. Sorry.'

Garret set his hands on his hips. 'Have you forgotten what today is? I've called the meeting for midday.'

'I haven't forgotten.' It was handover day. The day he'd slogged towards for years. The day all the hard work was supposed to pay off. But…

He held up an index finger. 'I'll be back in an hour.'

Garret's scowl deepened, then he grunted, 'Perhaps you shouldn't bother.'

On his way past, Mitch slowed up. 'What are you talking about—?'

'I'm talking about being worse than distracted in the board meeting this week. I'm talking about managers phoning or filing in to my office wondering what the hell's gotten into you. I'm talking about important clients who've claimed that you're preoccupied. One was so concerned, I had to talk him down from taking his business elsewhere.'

Mitch ploughed his hands into his pockets. 'Jasper Target?' Garret nodded. 'You know if Target's not complaining, he's not happy.'

'*I'm* not happy.'

He wouldn't admit it aloud, but Garret had a point; he *had* been distracted. And that was what he intended to sort out. 'I'll be back by midday.'

Shaking his head, Garret returned to his office and shut the door.

Mitch strode for the lift and half an hour later he was storming down Vanessa's drive. As luck would have it, she'd just come out of her flat and was walking towards him. On seeing her unexpected visitor, her face drained of colour.

Her mouth opened, then shut before she got out, 'What are you doing here?'

Feeling the connection—the immediate sizzle in his blood whenever she was near—he stopped before her. It had felt like a year since he'd held her, not a few days. 'I needed to see you.'

Her gaze dropping to her sandalled feet, she mumbled something unintelligible, then said more clearly, 'I'm going for more antibiotics. I'm still not well.'

His face hardened. She was lying.

Ignoring the ache low in his throat, he told her, 'Try again.'

With guilty eyes, she glanced over at a window; in his peripheral vision he saw a blind snap shut.

Then she looked him dead on and must have

known he meant business. Giving in, she expelled a worn-down sigh. 'I guess you need to know…'

He bit down against the pulse beating in his jaw. 'Guess I do.'

'I thought it was better we didn't see each other for a while.'

He counted to three—to ten—then raised his chin. 'Want to give me a reason?'

'You were having such an important time at work.'

His head kicked back. *Sorry?* 'And what does that have to do with anything?'

'I didn't want to get in the way of—' She dropped her gaze. 'Don't ask me, Mitch.'

Damn right he'd ask! 'What's going on, Vanessa?'

'I need to go.' She stepped around him.

But he caught her arm. 'The avoidance game's over. And, in case you're considering skimping, I want to know it all.'

She slumped and closed her eyes, as if she couldn't bear to see his face when she came clean.

'Your mother filled me in on your problems at work. She said you were in danger of losing the chair if…'

'If *what*?'

Her throat bobbed as she swallowed. 'If you continued to see me. Apparently I'm bad for your mental health.'

He didn't suppress his growl. He'd have it out with his mother later; this time she'd gone too far. But was he reading the rest of this story right?

He released his grip on her sleeve and tried to control some of his agitation by crossing his arms. 'Go on.'

'I decided it would be best if we didn't see each other until after your promotion was settled.'

'So you tried to be a pain in the butt last Sunday night to put me off?' She nibbled her lip and nodded. 'And to make sure I wouldn't be tempted, you pretended to be contagious.'

'I wanted you to be able to concentrate fully on your work. I didn't want to get in the way.'

'And lying and worrying me sick was the plan you came up with?'

She flinched. 'It doesn't sound very bright now.'

No, it really didn't. She'd had his best interests at heart—with her background, she wouldn't have had any experience with the scheming likes of his mother. But, *sweet blazes*, acting in a mature, logical manner and talking to him would've made far more sense, as well as saving a lot of angst. He cringed to think how she'd act in a real crisis.

Speaking of which…

He caught the time on his watch. He needed to get back and placate Garret. Garret wasn't to blame for being peeved over his protégé's recent preoccupations. Jasper Target was an extremely important client. Mitch had acted less than professionally.

It wouldn't happen again.

Vanessa touched his arm. 'I'm sorry. I didn't mean to make things worse.'

'It's not your fault.' He squeezed her hand then lowered it away. 'It's mine.'

'Because you should've trusted your instincts?' she ventured in a quiet voice.

He fought the urge to say, *Perhaps*.

Instead, he straightened his tie. 'I only know the most important meeting of my life is in fifteen minutes and I don't have any more time to waste. So—' he managed a tip of his head before turning away '—I'll let you go.'

'That sounds like goodbye.'

He stopped. Turned back.

He was annoyed. Angry. If he spoke now, chances were he'd make this mess worse. He'd rather let it slide.

And slide a little more.

When his BlackBerry beeped, he growled and headed off. 'I have to go.' He had to go *now*.

'Mitch, you didn't answer me.'

He wheeled back again. Counting his heartbeats, he held her glistening gaze with his. People relied on him. After today, the buck stopped with him. He couldn't afford to lose his head. On top of that, Ness wasn't comfortable in his world. Her discomfit at the charity cocktail party the other night had made that clear enough. They were good together—on one level. But on every other...

He held his breath.

Maybe it was kinder...

Maybe it was better...

To be tough.

He set his jaw and looked her in the eye while his heart dropped in his chest. 'Goodbye, Ness.'

Her pupils dilated before she exhaled and a wan,

close to accepting smile appeared. She nodded slowly. 'Bye, Mitch. Be sure to watch the rocks on your way out.'

When Mitch arrived back at the office and burst into the boardroom, a sombre Garret Jeffson glanced up from the end of the long table.

With bigger than usual bags under his eyes, the older man indicated the chair on his right. Then he sat back, tapping his pen on the notepad before him. 'Glad you could make it.'

Finger-combing his hair—he'd driven back with the top down—Mitch lowered into the chair. 'It's been a crazy couple of weeks.'

'Indeed. Do you anticipate the following weeks being as crazy?'

With his heartbeat pounding in his ears, Mitch held his breath, then shook his head. 'As of now, things are back to normal.'

Garret measured Mitch's expression for a long moment, as if looking for cracks, then retrieved a set of papers from his briefcase. 'It's all here, ready for your signature. Put your X on the dotted line and the chair's all yours.'

His hand slightly shaky, Mitch casually extracted the gold pen from the breast pocket of his jacket. After a token perusal of the document—he trusted Garret to have everything in perfect order—he initialled each page, then swept his signature over a final line and sat back.

Done.

After Garret witnessed the signature, he pushed back his chair. Mitch rose too, taking the older man's hand.

For the first time in weeks, Garret's smile looked sincere. 'Let me know how it goes.'

Waiting for the high to kick in, Mitch shook hands heartily. 'Will do.'

Garret nodded, collected his briefcase and headed for the door.

Mitch blinked. 'You're leaving now? I thought you might hang around and crack open a bottle of champagne to help celebrate.'

'Trudy's coming home from the hospital today. I promised—' Garret stopped himself and rephrased. 'I want to be there for her now.'

Mitch evaluated the man who'd taught him so much—hard lessons in life and business he would never forget. He shrugged. 'Guess that's it, then.'

'Good luck, son. Not that you'll need it. I was wrong to worry. This institution's your life. I should've known you wouldn't let the team down.' He lifted a brow. 'Doesn't mean you can't have a balance.'

As the door shut, Mitch thought over Garret's parting words, but then quickly pulled himself back. He might have finally reached the top, but that merely meant, more than ever, he needed to keep his eye on the game. Needed to keep his mind on the task. Balance was a luxury other people could afford.

Sweeping up the document, he strode down the hall and into his office. He shrugged off his jacket, swung it on the coat stand. But his determined expression slid as he peered around his massive penthouse office suite…the space on the wall where his portrait as President would hang…the piles of paperwork on his desk he would look through tonight.

He'd thought he'd feel different.

And he did.

He felt hollow.

CHAPTER TEN

THE following day, Vanessa sat cross-legged on the worn carpet in her shop's back room, her chin in her hand, her heart bleeding on the floor.

She'd tried to put Mitch out of her mind; she'd tried till three in the morning. But she simply couldn't do it. Their last conversation kept going round in her head. What he'd said, his expression, her replies, how she'd persisted, then she'd replay it all over again.

The repetition drove her mad, but she knew why she persisted. She was hoping that somehow the outcome would be different and, rather than goodbye, Mitch would declare his love. She'd imagined it. Her soul had *cried* for it.

Sad thing was, she didn't blame him. She hadn't wanted to deceive him, but she hadn't felt she'd had a choice. Staying out of his life had seemed the best bet; if she'd been upfront and told him about his mother's pointed chat, given his black mood towards Mr Jeffson on Sunday after receiving his message, she shuddered to think how the following days would have played out. She'd figured once he had Garret Jeffson off his back and the promotion in the bag, they could resume their relationship.

But she'd been caught out. Her absence from his life last week had caused more harm than good. He no longer trusted her.

No longer wanted her.

Knocking aside the tear falling down her cheek, Vanessa sucked in a breath and focused.

The fairy tale was over. She'd known it couldn't last. Too much had been against them. Now she was back to where and what she knew. These animals were her family. This was her home. Maybe one day a more realistic Prince Charming would come along.

But, after having Mitch, she honestly didn't see herself ever loving again.

She was playing with Roger, dangling a thread of orange wool which he pawed and chased, when Lucy interrupted.

'Miss Craig—' She amended, 'I mean Ness, a man's here. Says he's the landlord. He's with a lady.' Lucy hugged herself as if a chill had swept through the door. 'He doesn't look happy.'

Vanessa rose to her feet and put Roger back in his big corner pen with the others.

She'd left messages for her landlord and had asked him to return her calls; she wanted to speak with him about buying the shop. She was willing to pay more than the market price and, incorporated in the contract, they could tidy up the matter of outstanding rent.

Seemed they would start negotiations face to face.

Slipping on her shoes, she moved into the shop proper and held out her hand to her male guest. 'Hello, Mr Hodges.'

'Miss Craig.' Mr Hodges' bright red mop of hair wobbled on a curt nod. 'This is Mrs Ordiele. She's interested in taking over the lease.'

Mrs Ordiele forced herself away from running an approving eye over the clean, bright interior and popped out her hand. 'Great place. Absolutely ideal.'

Vanessa was still getting over Mr Hodges' statement; had he said this woman wanted to take over her lease?

'Thank you,' she replied to Mrs Ordiele's compliment. Then, to Mr Hodges, 'But something needs to be cleared up. I don't need to leave. Mr Hodges, I've left several messages—'

'But no money in the bank.' He looked slightly embarrassed for Mrs Ordiele's sake, but the willowy brunette was checking out the Lhasa Apsos.

Vanessa rubbed her palms down the outside of her jeans. 'About the rent…I actually wanted to speak with you about that.'

'Time for talk is over.' He sucked down a settling breath and his ruddy cheeks dropped a shade. 'Let's do this amicably, shall we? Without the bother of eviction notices and solicitors.'

'You don't understand.' Relishing the moment,

Vanessa squared her shoulders. 'I want to *buy* this shop.'

His expression froze before he laughed. 'I doubt you have that kind of money, Miss Craig.' He cocked a brow. 'Unless you've inherited a small fortune.'

'Name a price.'

He did—an amount she knew was too high.

'I'll put another twenty thousand on top of that,' she said, willing to go higher.

His tawny eyes sparkled, then narrowed. 'Thirty and it's yours.'

She stuck out her hand. 'Done.'

A delighted Mr Hodges crossed over to Mrs Ordiele. Vanessa saw the older woman's face drop when he spoke quietly and slid a glance back over his shoulder at the proud new owner.

Vanessa found a smile.

Me.

Lucy tapped her shoulder. 'There's a call for you, Ness.'

Vanessa wanted this moment to last. She might not have Mitch, but she'd achieved her earliest dream; soon she would own her own home. No one would ever take that away.

She threw a glance to Lucy. 'I'll call back.'

'It's about your aunt. The man sounded real upset.'

Vanessa studied Lucy's alarmed gaze, then rushed to grab the back extension.

Her heart was drumming in her throat when she asked of the receiver, 'Who is this?'

'Miss Craig? The name's Ernie Curtis. I purchased a painting from your aunt a few weeks ago. I believe she's left the country.'

Vanessa pulled the hair back from her damp brow and sat down. 'That's right.'

The man cleared his throat. 'This is a little embarrassing. I know she had no idea.'

Vanessa squeezed the receiver. 'What is it, Mr Curtis?'

'The painting…it's a replica. An incredibly good fake. I have no intention of bringing in the law. I know your aunt is a reputable woman.' He paused. 'I merely want my money back.'

The receiver slipped from her hand as every ounce of energy deserted her. She couldn't get her mouth to work and her fingers felt like rubber.

After a dazed moment, she bent and collected the phone.

'Miss Craig? Are you there?'

She moistened her lips but was unable to stop the spots from dancing before her eyes. 'I'm… sorry.'

'*Sorry?*'

He'd misunderstood. 'I mean—' her stomach wrenched '—of course you'll have your money back.'

She heard his expulsion of air. Relief. 'How can I contact your aunt?'

Vanessa pictured McKenzie—by the sink, loading washing, helping with homework, smiling proudly at birthdays. Last week had been the first time Vanessa had known McKenzie to put herself first, and even that was to see a sick friend.

The decision was unbearably painful but also explicitly clear.

She consciously released the tension locking her muscles. 'There's no need to contact my aunt. Give me your details and I'll wire your money through.'

Five minutes later, she found the strength to drag herself back out to her landlord, who was looking rather anxious and minus the chirpy Mrs Ordiele.

Vanessa stopped to look around.

Everything was hushed. Each animal, bird and fish seemed to be looking at her, waiting for the verdict. She'd already paid back Mitch's loan. She'd kept the correct amount from the cockapoos but had mailed back a cheque to Mrs Stuart for the surplus amount—the money Mrs Stuart had hoped she'd take to leave her son alone. Now she needed to pay back McKenzie's money.

Her guardian angel must have sent a saviour in Mrs Ordiele; she'd take over the care of this place and its boarders.

The pain of full understanding hit so strongly, she almost doubled over.

Oh, God, I have to leave.

After a few deep breaths, she joined the puzzled Mr Hodges to explain her changed circumstances. He could tell Mrs Ordiele the good news…

She was going to love it here.

CHAPTER ELEVEN

A WEEK later, Vanessa somehow found the strength to say farewell to Great and Small.

With her possessions removed, she said goodbye to her pets, to the male Rottie waiting to be collected, to Lucy, and finally to her kittens, who would soon be old enough to find their own homes.

Leaving Roger broke her heart. Had her landlord permitted cats, she'd have taken him with her. Instead she took solace in the knowledge that he was bound to lead a pampered fat cat life. She only wished it could've been with her.

When she walked out of the front door for the last time, feeling bedrock empty inside, she found herself heading to the steps of the Opera House.

Looking out over the silky blue water now, peering up at the wheeling gulls, she breathed in the briny air and wondered, *what next?* She'd had a couple of ideas, but she couldn't find enthusiasm for any of them. In fact, she dreaded nightfall because she worried she didn't have the wherewithal to even lift her butt off this step.

As if her memories weren't enough, the distant yap of a puppy caught her ear and the backs of her eyes prickled with fresh tears. Everywhere she looked—everything she saw or smelled or heard— kept bringing her back.

To what she'd lost.

To Mitch. Her home.

Where did she belong? Certainly not in his world; he'd made that choice for her. But today she felt utterly lost. As if she had no world of her own. No one at all.

Something wet bumped her elbow. She blinked and saw it was that excited puppy she must have heard barking before. A Rottweiler...

Heartbeat booming, she grabbed his panting face and looked into those happy chocolate-brown eyes. *Good grief.* 'Is that you, boy? You shouldn't be here.'

'He wanted to come visit.'

Vanessa's startled gaze shot up.

Mitch!

At his gorgeous crooked smile, she caught her runaway breath and a portion of her deep sadness slipped away, replaced by confusion. 'How did you find me? I don't understand.' She didn't understand any of it.

Had he heard about her misfortune and wanted to offer her another loan? If that was the case, thanks, but no thanks. That wasn't the answer.

Wearing that black wool-blend shirt she adored,

he sat down and lifted the dog onto his lap. 'I went to see you. Lucy filled me in on what happened. She told me that customer rang and said he no longer wanted this little guy. Then she mentioned you'd come here a few times this past week.' With next to no space between them and the pull of his magnetism so near, her skin began to heat. 'What'll you do?'

Although her head swam and her fingers itched to reach out and touch, she tried her best to digest what he'd told her and sound casual in her reply. 'I haven't decided. I might travel. Maybe Asia. More likely Greece.'

A dark brow jumped up. 'Plan to eat goat cheese and drink lemonade on a pebbled beach?'

After all the outstanding bills had been settled, thanks to the cockapoos, she'd had a little money left over. If she didn't make herself go now, perhaps she never would.

She deadpanned back, 'I don't see why not.'

'Me either.' His expression intensified. 'As long as I'm there too.'

Her pulse started to hammer and her cheeks began to burn. 'We've already said goodbye.' She didn't need to go through that again. Having her heart wrenched from her chest. Feeling as if tomorrow no longer mattered. She'd made a choice, perhaps a bad choice, to avoid his company that week; she was paying for it now. But she didn't need to hang around and suffer this added torture.

She pushed to her feet. 'I really have to go.'

He set the puppy down on his lead and stood too. 'Home?'

Outwardly cool, she shrugged. 'Probably.'

'We'll come too.'

She frowned. 'My landlord doesn't allow animals.'

'I'm talking about your shop.'

She obviously hadn't heard right. Or he'd misunderstood something. But then the sparkle in his eyes had her wondering.

Hoping.

'I heard your place was on the market for the right price,' he said.

'And you bought it?'

'I did.'

Tears filled her eyes, blurring her vision. The question she had to ask came out a squeak. 'But why?'

He smiled. 'Why do you think?'

She covered her mouth to block the emotion. This was too much. 'I can't do this right now.'

His face pinched as if he'd been slapped. 'Don't run away from me, Ness.'

She shut her eyes tight as desperate longing fisted in her chest. She didn't want to see his face or hear the words. It would only confuse her. And she didn't want to be confused again.

When she opened her eyes, he was still standing there, looking almost amused now.

'I suppose I could always kidnap you again,' he said.

She thought of that incredible night in his bed. How he'd held her. How he'd loved her.

Unwilling to be blinded again, she pointed out, 'That was a short-term solution.'

'And you want long-term.'

Her throat clogged up. 'What I *don't* want is to be toyed with. You got it right that first night, when you wanted to kiss me but decided to rip up my card instead.'

'Because I made an assumption,' he finished for her.

She tried to swallow the hurt. 'Yes.'

'Like I made another assumption last week.'

'No assumption. You and I had fun together. That's it.'

'I know.'

Taken aback, she looked at him harder. 'You do?'

'You like stories. Let me tell you one. After I left you the other day, I signed a paper and assumed control of an entity I thought would make me happy. It didn't. Instead, I felt angry. Unfulfilled. Frustrated. I needed to cool down, so I went back to our beach. I started to jog, to run, and then I was diving into the waves, swimming out. Way out. When the shoreline was a smudge, I realised what I was doing.'

She waited, breathless.

'Looking for sharks?'

'I was looking for my siren.'

She bit her inside cheek as a tear slipped down her face. 'You realise that the sailor in my story didn't succumb to the siren's call. His mates on the ship kept him tied up and he was saved.'

'Or damned?' His warm, strong hands found hers.

'I'd rather go on swimming and searching for ever than make a choice to go on living without you.' His voice lowered. 'I don't want to be married to my job. I want to be married to you. I want to have fun. I want to be your family. I'm ready. So are you.' As another salty trail ran into the corner of her mouth, his smile changed. 'I hurt you. I was wrong. Ness, I'm so sorry.'

She battled the raw emotion pushing up her throat. She was sorry too.

'Mitch…' She confessed, 'I couldn't bear to lose you again.'

'You won't have to.' His arms went around her and brought her close. 'From this moment on, I promise I'll be here. You don't have to worry about anyone else.'

'Your mother—'

'Knows she's beaten. Once she lowers her defences, she'll fall right in love with you. Just like I did.'

Her voice was a thready whisper. 'How do you know?'

'Know that I love you?' She nodded and his lips tugged. 'That's the easy part. I miss you. I laugh with you. I adore you. You're fabulous underwater.' She laughed and his smile widened. 'I could go on.'

Heck, he almost had her believing.

He cupped her face again and his essence swam out to embrace hers. 'I'm bewitched by you, Ness. Be my wife.' His expression sobered to an earnestness she'd never seen before. 'I love you with everything I've been or will ever be. Will we give us a go? What do you say?'

After that heartfelt affirmation, there was only one thing she *could* say.

She filled her lungs and dived in. 'I love you too. Seems like I always have.'

By the smile glowing in his eyes, she might have given him the only prize worth having.

He set his forehead on hers. 'You can be you. I'll be me, and we'll invent our own world. The very *best* world.'

When his mouth dropped over hers, and his promise-filled heat held her close, Vanessa knew to her soul it was true. Theirs would not only be the best.

Theirs would be for ever.

EPILOGUE

'It's settled. We're having moussaka for dinner.'

With eyes closed and one cheek resting on her crossed forearms, Vanessa roused herself at the rich, deep tones of her husband's voice. Giving a lazy stretch and rolling over, she blinked sleepily as a flock of sparrows darted and swooped across the endless azure sky.

The scent of orange blossom and wild oregano drifted in on a warm breeze, and if Mitch hadn't been standing above her—hands low on his hips, his sexy smile electrifyingly real—she'd have known that lying on the deck of a private yacht, moored in the cool blue waters off a popular Greek island, must be a dream.

Blissfully content, she reached out her arms to him. 'Perhaps we should stay on board tonight.'

She was still more than satisfied by the charcoal fire barbecue, baklava and strong Greek coffee they'd enjoyed early this afternoon at that gorgeous taverna. Hidden within a labyrinth of narrow cobblestone lanes laced with pink bougainvillea, she'd felt as if she'd entered another world. A world she'd longed to experience and was now enjoying on her honeymoon.

In chinos, rolled to his shins, and no shirt, Mitch made himself comfortable, lying beside her on the plush double towel. Warmed right the way through, she snuggled into his hard, bronzed chest and sighed as his strong arm drew her near.

He growled playfully as his lips grazed her temple and his natural scent joined with the other delights awakening her senses, feeding her soul.

'I'm more than happy staying put,' he said. 'All I need is some cheese, fresh bread—' he nuzzled her neck '—and a whole pile of you.'

His lips drifted over her jaw, sparking a trail of desire, which ignited and blew flames through her blood when his mouth covered hers. The roughness of his chin working languidly near her cheek…the rhythm of his breathing speeding up along with hers…

The kiss was deep and lasting—the kind of kiss poets wrote about and lonely people pined for.

She was lonely no more.

After a six-month engagement, they'd married two weeks ago in a ceremony that celebrated both tradition and individuality. The giant fairy-tale marquee had held over two hundred guests and offered a smorgasbord of cuisines from around the world. All of Mitch's family had been happy for them—including his mother. It had seemed good timing that, a week after Mitch's marriage proposal, Mrs Stuart had begun seeing a reclusive multimillionaire, who had instantly fallen for her 'frailty' and charm, and now doted on her every whim.

Josie and Tia had made beautiful bridesmaids, and Vanessa was thrilled that their guests had included Aunt McKenzie and her now fiancé, Jim, who had recovered enough from his respiratory illness to fly from L.A. to Australia. Around 10:00 p.m., the bride had kicked off her shoes; the dancing had lasted till long past midnight.

Now, as their lips softly parted, Vanessa enjoyed the high of her giddy heartbeat as she remembered their special day—the day she'd become Mitch Stuart's wife. But as the whitewashed houses dotting the craggy hillside in the distance caught her eye, she felt a twinge.

Homesickness.

Mitch's brow pinched before his fingertip weaved up her thigh. 'Let me guess. You're missing the shop?'

Her mouth swung to one side. 'Silly, huh.'

'No, not silly. But remember that Lucy was beside herself that you entrusted her with its running while we were gone.' He tickled her ribs. 'And we still have another couple of weeks before finding out whether our tender to buy the rest of that block is successful.'

A couple of weeks before the wedding, she'd mentioned her fantasy of expanding the store—but *her* way, with her own vet, grooming facilities and heaps more pets who needed good homes. Mitch hadn't hesitated in putting a bid for the entire string of shops into motion.

She stole a quick kiss and stayed close. 'You certainly know how to make a girl's dreams come true.'

He chuckled. 'Absolutely my pleasure.'

It seemed as if they had it all. The balance. The best of both worlds.

Well, almost.

She'd never allowed herself to think too deeply about the possibility of becoming a mother. Guess there'd been a part of her that had been afraid of a commitment she would take more seriously, and cherish more dearly, than any other. But now…

She sat up, then, cheeks heating, lowered her gaze. 'Mitch, I want to run something by you.'

'Another business venture?'

'This is strictly personal.'

His mouth caressed the sensitive inside crease of her arm. 'Tell me more.'

Her heartbeat raced as she voiced an idea that had grown so strong, she could no longer contain it. 'What would say to an adoption?'

His eyebrows jumped. 'Not another cat.'

'Mitch…I mean a *baby*.'

His head kicked back. His startling blue eyes had never looked wider.

'There are so many who need a good home,' she hurried on, 'and two loving parents who can give so much. I haven't changed my mind about having our own children, like we talked about. But I didn't think that should cancel out an adoption…or two.'

At his frozen expression, her spirits dropped and she hugged onto her knees. 'It was just an idea.'

His eyes began to sparkle, as mesmerising as the

surrounding sequinned blue sea. 'And possibly the best idea you've ever had.'

She let his words sink in. 'You think so? You *really* do?'

When he nodded, she threw her arms around his neck. Her heart felt so full, she wondered if it might burst. Now her secret wish was out and he'd agreed, she felt as if this moment of immeasurable joy had always been her destiny. A natural progression. The smiley-face icing on her cake.

With happy tears edging her eyes, she finally released him. 'We'll look into it as soon as we get back?' she asked.

'The very minute we get back,' he replied.

She melted as his hot fingers curved around her nape to draw her mouth to his. But when, over his shoulder, she saw something jump in the water, she pulled back and shielded her eyes against the glare. 'Did you see that?'

As a donkey brayed in the distance, he sat up taller too and glanced around. 'See what?'

'I think it's a dolphin.'

'Or possibly a mermaid?' He shrugged at her dry look. 'Hey, you never know.'

But she did know one thing. When they'd met, she'd wanted a home; Mitch had wanted fun. Now they had both, wrapped up in the beautiful big ribbon of their everlasting love.

Leaning in, she rubbed the tip of her nose with his.

'Guess what?' she murmured.

'What?' He smiled back.

'I feel happier—more in love—every day.'

The commitment in his eyes held her still before he gathered her close again.

'Oh, baby, so do I.'

* * * * *

Turn the page for an exclusive extract from
THE PRINCE'S CAPTIVE WIFE
by
Marion Lennox

Bedded and wedded—by blackmail!

Nine years ago Prince Andreas Karedes left Australia to inherit his royal duties, but unbeknownst to him he left a woman pregnant.

Innocent young Holly tragically lost their baby and remained on her parents' farm to be near her tiny son's final resting place, wishing Andreas would return!

A royal scandal is about to break: a dirt-digging journalist has discovered Holly's secret, so Andreas forces his childhood sweetheart to come and face him! Passion runs high as Andreas issues an ultimatum: to avoid scandal, Holly must become his royal bride!

"She was only seventeen?"

"We're talking ten years ago. I was barely out of my teens myself."

"Does that make a difference?" The uncrowned king of Aristo stared across his massive desk at his younger brother, his aquiline face dark with fury. "Have we not had enough scandal?"

"Not of my making." Prince Andreas Christos Karedes, third in line to the Crown of Aristo, stood his ground against his older brother with the disdain he always used in this family of testosterone-driven males. His father and brothers might be acknowledged womanizers, but Andreas made sure his affairs were discreet.

"Until now," Sebastian said. "Not counting your singularly spectacular divorce, which had a massive impact. But this is worse. You will have to sort it before it explodes over all of us."

"How the hell can I sort it?"

"Get rid of her."

"You're not saying…"

"Kill her?" Sebastian smiled up at his younger brother, obviously rejecting the idea—though a tinge of regret in his voice said the option wasn't altogether unattractive.

And Andreas even sympathized. Since their father's death, all three brothers had been dragged through the mire of the media spotlight, and the political unrest was threatening to destroy them. In their thirties, impossibly handsome, wealthy beyond belief, indulged and feted, the brothers were now facing realities they had no idea what to do with.

"Though if I was our father…" Sebastian added, and Andreas shuddered. Who knew what the old king would have done if he'd discovered Holly's secret? Thank God he'd never found out. Not that King Aegeus could have taken the moral high ground. It was, after all, his father's past actions that had gotten them into this mess.

"You'll make a better king than our father ever was," Andreas said softly. "What filthy dealing made him dispose of the royal diamond?"

"That's my concern," Sebastian said. There could be no royal coronation until the diamond was found—they all knew that—but the way the media was baying for blood there might not be a coronation even then. Without the diamond the rules had changed. If any more scandals broke… "This girl…"

"Holly."

"You remember her?"

"Of course I remember her."

"Then she'll be easy to find. We'll buy her off—do whatever it takes, but she mustn't talk to anyone."

"If she wanted to make a scandal she could have done it years ago."

"So it's been simmering in the wings for years. To have it surface now…" Sebastian rose and fixed Andreas with a look that was almost as deadly as the one used by the old king. "It can't happen, brother. We have to make sure she's not in a position to bring us down."

"I'll contact her."

"You'll go nowhere near her until we're sure of her reaction. Not even a phone call, brother. For all we know her phones are already tapped. I'll have her brought here."

"I can arrange…"

"You stay right out of it until she's on our soil. You're heading the corruption inquiry. With Alex on his honeymoon with Maria—of all the times for him to demand to marry, this must surely be the worst—I need you more than ever. If you leave now and this leaks, we can almost guarantee losing the crown."

"So how do you propose to persuade her to come?"

"Oh, I'll persuade her," Sebastian said grimly. "She's only a slip of a girl. She might be your past, but there's no way she's messing with our future."

* * * * *

Be sure to look for
THE PRINCE'S CAPTIVE WIFE
by Marion Lennox,
available September 2009
from Harlequin Presents®!

HARLEQUIN *Presents*

TWO CROWNS, TWO ISLANDS, ONE LEGACY

A royal family, torn apart by pride and its lust for power, reunited by purity and passion

THE ROYAL HOUSE *of* KAREDES

Pick up the next adventures in this passionate series!

THE PRINCE'S CAPTIVE WIFE
by Marion Lennox, September 2009

THE SHEIKH'S FORBIDDEN VIRGIN
by Kate Hewitt, October 2009

THE GREEK BILLIONAIRE'S INNOCENT PRINCESS
by Chantelle Shaw, November 2009

THE FUTURE KING'S LOVE-CHILD
by Melanie Milburne, December 2009

RUTHLESS BOSS, ROYAL MISTRESS
by Natalie Anderson, January 2010

THE DESERT KING'S HOUSEKEEPER BRIDE
by Carol Marinelli, February 2010

www.eHarlequin.com

HP12851

HARLEQUIN *Presents*

International Billionaires

Life is a game of power and pleasure.
And these men play to win!

THE VIRGIN SECRETARY'S IMPOSSIBLE BOSS
by **Carole Mortimer**

Billionaire Linus loves a challenge.
During one snowbound Scottish night
the temperature rises with his sensible
personal assistant. With sparks flying,
how can Andi resist?

Book #2854

Available September 2009

HPI2854

REQUEST YOUR FREE BOOKS!

HARLEQUIN® *Presents*®

2 FREE NOVELS
PLUS 2
FREE GIFTS!

PASSION GUARANTEED SEDUCTION

YES! Please send me 2 FREE Harlequin Presents® novels and my 2 FREE gifts (gifts are worth about $10). After receiving them, if I don't wish to receive any more books, I can return the shipping statement marked "cancel". If I don't cancel, I will receive 6 brand-new novels every month and be billed just $4.05 per book in the U.S. or $4.74 per book in Canada. That's a savings of close to 15% off the cover price! It's quite a bargain! Shipping and handling is just 50¢ per book*. I understand that accepting the 2 free books and gifts places me under no obligation to buy anything. I can always return a shipment and cancel at any time. Even if I never buy another book, the two free books and gifts are mine to keep forever.

106 HDN EYRQ 306 HDN EYR2

Name _____ (PLEASE PRINT) _____

Address _____ Apt. # _____

City _____ State/Prov. _____ Zip/Postal Code _____

Signature (if under 18, a parent or guardian must sign) _____

Mail to the **Harlequin Reader Service:**
IN U.S.A.: P.O. Box 1867, Buffalo, NY 14240-1867
IN CANADA: P.O. Box 609, Fort Erie, Ontario L2A 5X3

Not valid to current subscribers of Harlequin Presents books.

Are you a current subscriber of Harlequin Presents books and want to receive the larger-print edition? Call 1-800-873-8635 today!

HP09R

TAKEN: AT THE BOSS'S COMMAND

His every demand will *be met!*

Whether he's a British billionaire, an Argentinian
polo player, an Italian tycoon or a Greek magnate,
these men demand the very best of everything—
and everyone....

Working with him is one thing—marrying him is *quite*
another. But when the boss chooses his bride,
there's no option but to say I do!

**Catch all the heart-racing stories,
available September 2009:**

The Boss's Inexperienced Secretary #69
by HELEN BROOKS

Argentinian Playboy,
Unexpected Love-Child #70
by CHANTELLE SHAW

The Tuscan Tycoon's
Pregnant Housekeeper #71
by CHRISTINA HOLLIS

Kept by Her Greek Boss #72
by KATHRYN ROSS

I ♥

HARLEQUIN® *Presents*
